'I love reading Simenon. He makes me think of Chekhov'
– William Faulkner

'A truly wonderful writer . . . marvellously readable – lucid, simple, absolutely in tune with the world he creates'
– Muriel Spark

'Few writers have ever conveyed with such a sure touch, the bleakness of human life'
– A. N. Wilson

'One of the greatest writers of the twentieth century . . . Simenon was unequalled at making us look inside, though the ability was masked by his brilliance at absorbing us obsessively in his stories'
– *Guardian*

'A novelist who entered his fictional world as if he were part of it'
– Peter Ackroyd

'The greatest of all, the most genuine novelist we have had in literature'
– André Gide

'Superb . . . The most addictive of writers . . . A unique teller of tales'
– *Observer*

'The mysteries of the human personality are revealed in all their disconcerting complexity'
– Anita Brookner

'A writer who, more than any other crime novelist, combined a high literary reputation with popular appeal'
– P. D. James

'A supreme writer . . . Unforgettable vividness'
– *Independent*

'Compelling, remorseless, brilliant'
– John Gray

'Extraordinary masterpieces of the twentieth century'
– John Banville

Georges Simenon was born on 12 February 1903 in Liège, Belgium, and died in 1989 in Lausanne, Switzerland, where he had lived for the latter part of his life. Between 1931 and 1972 he published seventy-five novels and twenty-eight short stories featuring Inspector Maigret. *Maigret and Monsieur Charles* marks the end of the series – and Simenon's career as a novelist. He describes the moment when he sat down to write his next novel and realized there would be no more:

> At the beginning of February . . . I had written *Maigret et Monsieur Charles*, not knowing that it would be my final novel . . .

> September 18 I go down to my office to set up the yellow folder for a new novel. I close my door at 9.00 am. I have to set down the names of my characters, their résumés, their ancestry, sometimes their childhood friends, all the pertinent information . . . It would not work out.

Penguin has published the entire series of Maigret novels.

GEORGES SIMENON

Maigret and Monsieur Charles

Translated by ROS SCHWARTZ

PENGUIN BOOKS

PENGUIN CLASSICS

UK | USA | Canada | Ireland | Australia
India | New Zealand | South Africa

Penguin Books is part of the Penguin Random House group of companies
whose addresses can be found at global.penguinrandomhouse.com.

First published in serial, as *Maigret et M. Charles*, in *Le Figaro* 1972
First published in book form by Presses de la Cité 1972
This translation first published 2020

006

Set in 12.5/15 pt Dante MT Std
Typeset by Jouve (UK), Milton Keynes
Printed and bound in Great Britain by Clays Ltd, Elcograf S.p.A.

ISBN: 978–0–241–30441–9

www.greenpenguin.co.uk

Maigret and Monsieur Charles

1.

In a still timid ray of March sunshine, Maigret was playing. He was playing not with building blocks, like when he was a child, but with pipes.

There were always five or six on his desk and, each time he filled one, he had carefully selected it to suit his mood.

His gaze was vague, his shoulders hunched. He had just decided on the future of his career. He had no regrets, but even so he felt a certain sadness.

Mechanically, and with the utmost seriousness, he arranged the pipes on his blotting pad to create geometric or animal shapes.

The morning's post sat in a pile on the right-hand side of the desk, but he had no wish to deal with it.

On his arrival at the Police Judiciaire just before nine that morning, he had found a summons from the prefect of police, which was rare, and he'd gone to Boulevard du Palais wondering what it boded.

The prefect had received him at once, cordial and smiling.

'Can you guess why I wanted to see you?'

'I have to admit I can't.'

'Have a seat and light your pipe.'

The prefect was young, barely forty, a graduate from an elite university. He was stylish, perhaps a little too stylish.

'You are aware that the head of the Police Judiciaire will be retiring next month after being in post for twelve years . . . I discussed his replacement yesterday with the interior minister, and we were both agreed that we should offer the position to you . . .'

The prefect was probably expecting to see Maigret's face light up with pleasure.

But on the contrary, Maigret looked downcast.

'Is that an order?' he asked, almost grumpily.

'No, of course not, but you must appreciate that it is an important promotion, the biggest step up that an official of the Police Judiciaire can hope for . . .'

'I know. But all the same, I'd rather stay head of the Crime Squad. Please don't take my reply the wrong way. I've been an active police officer for forty years, and I'd find it hard to spend my days in an office, studying files and dealing with administrative matters . . .'

The prefect did not conceal his surprise.

'Why don't you take some time to think it over and give me your answer in a few days? You might also wish to discuss it with Madame Maigret.'

'She would understand.'

'I understand too, and I don't want to press the matter . . .'

Even so, he appeared slightly disappointed. He understood without understanding. Maigret needed the human contact his investigations afforded him, and he'd often been criticized for not conducting them from his desk, choosing instead to play an active role and undertaking tasks that were usually carried out by inspectors.

He toyed with his pipes, his mind a blank. The latest arrangement reminded him of a stork.

The window sparkled in the sunlight. The prefect had shown him to the door and shaken his hand warmly. Even so, Maigret knew that his superiors would be annoyed.

He slowly lit one of his pipes and smoked it in little puffs.

Within minutes, he'd decided his future, in the short term anyway, because, in three years' time, he would have to retire. At least let him spend those three years as he pleased, for goodness' sake!

He needed to get out of his office, soak up the atmosphere and discover different worlds with each new investigation. He needed the cafés and bars where he so often ended up waiting, at the counter, drinking a beer or a calvados depending on the circumstances.

He needed to do battle patiently in his office with a suspect who refused to talk and sometimes, after hours and hours, to obtain a dramatic confession.

He felt queasy. He was afraid that, on reflection, he would be forced to accept this appointment, one way or another. But he didn't want it at any price, even though it was a sort of badge of honour.

He stared at the pipes, occasionally moving them like the pieces on a chessboard. He jumped when he heard discreet taps on the door between his office and that of the inspectors.

Without waiting for a reply, Lapointe came in.

'Sorry to disturb you, chief—'

'You're not disturbing me at all.'

It was now nearly ten years since Lapointe had joined the Police Judiciaire and he'd been nicknamed 'young Lapointe'. He'd been thin and lanky in those days. Since then, he'd filled out a bit. He had married and had two children. But the nickname had stuck and some called him 'Maigret's little puppy'.

'There's a woman in my office who is adamant she must see you in person. She won't say a word to me. She's sitting bolt upright, absolutely still, and is determined to have her way.'

This often happened. Because of articles in the press, people insisted on seeing him and only him and it was often difficult to get them to change their minds. Some even came to his apartment in Boulevard Richard-Lenoir – goodness knows how they had managed to get hold of his home address.

'Did she give you her name?'

'Here's her card.'

Madame Sabin-Levesque
207a, Boulevard Saint-Germain

'I find her strange,' said Lapointe. 'She stares straight ahead and has a sort of twitch that pulls down the right-hand corner of her mouth. She hasn't taken her gloves off, but you can see her fingers are clenched.'

'Show her in and stay here. Grab your notebook, just in case.'

Maigret looked at his pipes and heaved a rueful sigh. Playtime was over.

When the woman entered, he rose to his feet.

'Please have a seat, madame . . .'

Her eyes bored into him.

'You are Detective Chief Inspector Maigret, are you not?'

'Yes.'

'I imagined you fatter.'

She was wearing a fur coat and matching hat. Was it mink? Maigret had no idea, because the wife of a divisionary chief inspector generally had to be content with rabbit or, at best, muskrat or nutria.

Madame Sabin-Levesque's eyes roved slowly around the office as if making an inventory. When Lapointe sat down at the end of the desk, with his notebook and pencil, she asked:

'Is this young man going to stay in the room?'

'Of course.'

'Is he going to make a note of our conversation?'

'It's the rule.'

Her brow furrowed and she gripped her crocodile-skin handbag tighter.

'I thought I'd be able to speak with you in private.'

Maigret did not reply. He observed his customer and, like Lapointe, found her odd, to say the least. Sometimes her gaze was disturbingly fixed, and sometimes she seemed absent.

'I presume you know who I am?'

'I read your name on your card.'

'Do you know who my husband is?'

'I expect he has the same name as you.'

'He's one of the most prominent lawyers in Paris.'

Her lips kept twitching, one corner of her mouth turning down, trembling. She seemed to be finding it hard to remain composed.

'Please continue.'

'He has disappeared.'

'In that case, I'm not the right person to talk to. There's a special missing persons department.'

She gave a joyless, ironic smile, and didn't bother to reply.

It was difficult to guess her age. She couldn't be much more than forty, forty-five at most, but her face bore the signs of suffering and her eyes were puffy.

'Did you drink before coming here?' Maigret suddenly asked.

'Is that of interest to you?'

'Yes. You're the one who insisted on seeing me, aren't you? You should expect questions that you may feel are indiscreet.'

'I thought you would be different. More understanding.'

'It is precisely because I try to understand that I need to know certain things.'

'I had two glasses of brandy, to give myself courage.'

'Only two?'

She looked at him but said nothing.

'When did your husband go missing?'

'Over a month ago. On the 18th of February. Today's the 21st of March . . .'

'Did he tell you he was going away?'

'He didn't breathe a word to me.'

'And it's taken you all this time to report his disappearance?'

'I'm used to it.'

'To what?'

'To him disappearing for a few days.'

'Has this been going on for long?'

'Years. It began shortly after our marriage, fifteen years ago.'

'He doesn't give you any reason for these trips?'

'I don't think he actually goes away.'

'I don't understand.'

'He stays in Paris or in the area.'

'How do you know?'

'Because, the first few times, I had him followed by a private detective. I stopped because it was always the same thing.'

Her speech was slurred and it wasn't just two glasses of brandy that she'd drunk. Nor had it been to give herself courage, because her ravaged face and her struggle to maintain her composure revealed that she was a hardened drinker.

'I'm waiting for you to give me some details.'

'My husband is like that.'

'Like what?'

'He gets swept off his feet. He meets a woman he fancies and feels the urge to live with her for a few days. Until now his longest fling, as it were, lasted two weeks.'

'You're not going to tell me that he picked them up in the street?'

'Almost. Usually in nightclubs.'

'Did he go out alone?'

'Always.'

'He never took you with him?'

'We haven't meant anything to each other for a long time.'

'Even so, you are worried.'

'About him.'

'Not about yourself?'

There was a steely glint of defiance in her eyes.

'No.'

'You don't love him any more?'

'No.'

'What about him, does he love you?'

'Even less.'

'But you still live together.'

'The apartment is large. We keep different hours, so we don't often run into each other.'

Lapointe was taking notes with surprise written all over his face.

'Why have you come here?'

'So that you can find him.'

'Were you never worried in the past?'

'A month is a long time. He didn't take anything with him, not even a small suitcase or clean underwear. And he didn't take one of the cars either.'

'Do you own several cars?'

'Two. The Bentley, which he takes most frequently, and the Fiat, which is more or less for my use.'

'Do you drive?'

'The chauffeur, Vittorio, drives me when I go out.'

'Do you go out a lot?'

'Nearly every afternoon.'

'To meet up with women friends?'

'I don't have any friends . . .'

He had rarely encountered such a bitter and disconcerting woman.

'Do you go shopping?'

'I hate shopping.'

'Do you go for walks in the Bois de Boulogne or elsewhere?'

'I go to the cinema.'

'Every day?'

'Almost. When I'm not too tired.'

As with drug addicts, there came a moment when she needed a fix, and that moment had come. It was obvious that she'd have given anything for a glass of brandy, but Maigret could hardly offer her one, even though there was a bottle in his cupboard for certain occasions that arose. He felt a little sorry for her.

'I am trying to understand, Madame Sabin.'

'Sabin-Levesque,' she corrected him.

'As you prefer. Has your husband always been in the habit of absconding for days at a time?'

'Never for an entire month.'

'You already said so.'

'I have a premonition.'

'What premonition?'

'I'm afraid that something's happened to him . . .'

'Do you have a reason for thinking that?'

'No. You don't need a reason to have a premonition.'

'You say your husband is a prominent lawyer.'

'Let us say that he has a very large firm and one of the most prestigious clienteles in Paris.'

'How can he take leave so frequently?'

'Gérard does as little legal work as possible. He inherited the firm from his father, but it's mainly the chief clerk who deals with things . . .'

'I have the impression you are tired?'

'I'm always tired. I am in poor health.'

'What about your husband?'

'At forty-eight, he's like a young man.'

'If I understand correctly, we're likely to learn about his movements from the nightclubs . . .'

'I think so.'

Maigret was pensive. He felt as if his questions were on the wrong track and that the answers he received were leading nowhere.

At one point, he wondered whether he was in the presence of a madwoman, or in any case, a neurotic. He'd seen a number of them in his office over the years, and most of them had made his life difficult.

The words she spoke sounded normal, plausible; at the same time, there seemed to be a discrepancy between them and reality.

'Do you think he had a lot of money on him?'

'As far as I know, he generally used his cheque book.'

'Have you discussed it with the chief clerk?'

'We are not on speaking terms.'

'Why not?'

'Because, around three years ago, my husband banned me from his office.'

'Did he have a reason?'

'I have no idea.'

'You are on bad terms with the chief clerk, but even so, you must know him?'

'Lecureur – that's his name – has always disapproved of me.'

'Was he already part of the firm when your father-in-law died?'

'He joined at the age of twenty-two.'

'Might he have a better idea of your husband's whereabouts?'

'It's possible. But if I were to go and ask him, he wouldn't say anything . . .'

That twitch again, which was beginning to irritate Maigret. He had the growing feeling that this interview was an ordeal for his visitor. So why had she come?

'Which kind of marriage contract do you have?'

'We were married under the convention of separate assets.'

'Do you have a personal fortune?'

'No.'

'Does your husband give you all the money you need?'

'Yes. He's not interested in money. I can't swear to it, but I think he's very wealthy.'

Maigret asked questions at random. He was trying all avenues but, so far, he'd drawn a blank.

'Look, you're exhausted. Understandably. With your permission, I'll come and see you at home, this afternoon . . .'

'As you wish.'

She hadn't stood up yet but was still fiddling with her handbag.

'What do you think of me?' she asked at last, in a flat voice.

'I don't think anything for now.'

'You find me difficult, don't you?'

'Not necessarily.'

'At school the other girls found me difficult and I've never had any female friends to speak of.'

'And yet you are very clever.'

'Do you think so?'

She gave a smile, her lips trembling.

'It hasn't done me any good.'

'Have you never been happy?'

'Never. I don't know what the word means.'

She pointed to Lapointe, who was still taking notes.

'Is it really essential for this conversation to be recorded? It's hard to speak freely when someone's noting down everything you say.'

'If there's something you want to tell me in confidence, we'll stop taking notes.'

'I don't have anything more to say right now . . .'

She struggled to her feet. Her shoulders drooped and her back was slightly hunched, her chest hollow.

'Does he have to come with you this afternoon?'

Maigret hesitated, wanting to give her a chance.

'I'll come alone.'

'At what time?'

'Whenever is best for you.'

'I normally take a nap. Would four o'clock suit you?'

'Perfectly.'

'It's on the first floor. Take the right-hand door under the arch.'

She did not hold out her hand. She walked stiffly over to the door as if she were afraid of falling over.

'Thank you all the same for seeing me,' she muttered grudgingly.

And, after one last look at Maigret, she made her way towards the main staircase.

The two men stared at one other as if they were each waiting for the other to speak first. The difference was that Lapointe looked bewildered whereas Maigret was solemn but with a roguish glint in his eyes.

He went to open the window, then filled the rather fat pipe he'd selected. Lapointe couldn't contain himself any longer.

'What do you think, chief?'

It was a question that his colleagues rarely ventured to ask him because he generally replied with a grunt that had become familiar: 'I don't think.'

This time, he responded with another question:

'About this business of the missing husband?'

'More about her . . .'

Maigret lit his pipe, stationed himself in front of the window and, contemplating the banks of the Seine bathed in sunlight, sighed:

'She's a strange woman . . .'

Nothing else. He didn't try to analyse his impressions, let alone put them into words. Lapointe gathered that he was perturbed and regretted having asked his question so impetuously.

'She might be mad,' he added anyway.

And Maigret gave him a brooding look, without saying a word.

He stayed by the window for a good while, then said:

'Will you have lunch with me?'

'I'd be delighted, chief. Especially since my wife is at her sister's, in Saint-Cloud.'

'Let's say in fifteen minutes.'

Lapointe went out. Maigret called the switchboard and requested Boulevard Richard-Lenoir.

'Is that you?' queried his wife's voice before he had opened his mouth.

'It's me.'

'I bet you're going to tell me that you're not coming home for lunch.'

'You guessed right.'

'Brasserie Dauphine?'

'With Lapointe.'

'A new case?'

Three weeks earlier, he'd concluded his previous investigation and this desire for lunch in Place Dauphine was a sign of his pleasure in resuming active service. It was also a little like thumbing his nose at the prefect and the interior minister, who'd taken it into their heads to shut him away in a lavish office.

'Yes.'

'I haven't seen anything in the newspapers.'

'The press hasn't written about it yet and might not do so.'

'Well, enjoy it. I was only going to offer you grilled herring . . .'

He stood there thinking for a moment, then picked up the telephone again, staring at the chair in which the visitor had sat. He could picture her, with her edginess, her shining eyes and nervous twitch.

'Put me through to Maître Demaison, would you?'

He knew that at this hour the lawyer would be at home.

'Maigret here.'

'How are you? Have you got some poor wretch of a murderer who needs defending?'

'Not yet. I simply need some information. Do you know a lawyer called Sabin-Levesque, Boulevard Saint-Germain?'

'Gérard? Indeed I do. We were at law school together.'

'What do you think of him?'

'Has he run off again?'

'You're in the know?'

'All his friends are in the know. From time to time, he gets swept off his feet by a pretty woman and disappears for a night or for a few days. He has a pronounced taste for what I would call semi-professionals – strip-tease artists, for example, or nightclub hostesses . . .'

'Does it happen often?'

'About ten times a year, as far as I'm aware . . .'

'Is he a competent lawyer?'

'He inherited one of the most prestigious clienteles in Paris, almost the entire Faubourg Saint-Germain, even though he bears no resemblance to a conventional lawyer. He wears light-coloured suits, and sometimes loud checked tweed jackets.

'He's a very cheerful character, full of life, who always looks on the bright side, which doesn't prevent him from managing the business entrusted to him with outstanding flair . . .

'I know several of his clients, male and female, who swear by him . . .'

'Do you know his wife?'

A pregnant pause.

'Yes.'

'And?'

'She's a strange person. I wouldn't like to live with her, and most likely neither does Gérard, because he sees as little of her as possible.'

'Does she sometimes go out with him?'

'Not as far as I know.'

'Does she have women friends, men friends?'

'Not to my knowledge either.'

'Lovers?'

'I haven't heard any gossip about her. Most people take her for a depressive or a madwoman. She drinks like a fish.'

'I noticed.'

'I've told you everything I know.'

'Apparently the husband's been missing for a month.'

'And no one's heard from him?'

'It seems not. That's why she's worried and came to see me this morning.'

'Why you and not the missing persons' bureau?'

'That's what I asked. She didn't reply.'

'Usually, when he disappears for a few days, he stays in

telephone contact with his chief clerk, whose name I've forgotten . . . Have you talked to him?'

'I'll probably see him this afternoon . . .'

A few minutes later, Maigret opened the door to the inspectors' office and beckoned to Lapointe, who hastened over with a certain awkwardness which he couldn't help in Maigret's presence. Maigret was his idol.

'No need for an overcoat,' muttered his chief. 'We're only going round the corner.'

That morning, he had put on a light spring coat, which was hanging from the hook.

Their footsteps echoed on the pavement. It was good to be back in the atmosphere of the Brasserie Dauphine with its aromas of cooking and alcohol. At the bar were several police officers and Maigret waved to them.

He and Lapointe went straight into the cosy restaurant with its view over the Seine.

The owner shook their hands.

'A little pastis to welcome the spring?'

Maigret hesitated and ended up saying yes. Lapointe did likewise and the owner brought the glasses.

'An investigation?'

'Probably.'

'Mind you, I'm not asking any questions . . . You can count on me, I'll keep it under my hat . . . What would you say to sweetbreads with mushrooms . . . ?'

Maigret savoured his pastis, because he hadn't drunk one for a long time. They were served some appetizers.

'I wonder whether she'll be more talkative this afternoon when I'm not there.'

'I'm wondering the same thing . . .'

They ate a relaxed meal rounded off with the almond cake made by the owner's wife, who served it in person, after wiping her hands on her apron.

It was not yet two o'clock when the two men walked up the stairs of the Police Judiciaire.

'They've modernized the building,' grumbled Maigret, out of breath, 'but it didn't occur to them to put in a lift.'

He went into his office, lit a pipe and started sifting through his post without much interest. It mainly comprised administrative forms to be completed and reports to be countersigned. The time dragged. Occasionally, he looked out of the window and mentally escaped from the office.

For once, spring had arrived on time. The air was limpid, the sky a pale blue and the buds already swelling. In a few days' time, the first tender green leaves would appear.

'I don't know when I'll be back,' he announced from the inspectors' doorway.

He had decided to make his way to Boulevard Saint-Germain on foot, but he regretted it because it felt like a long walk to number 207a and he had to mop his brow several times.

The imposing stone building, which had turned grey over time, resembled most of the apartment buildings on the boulevard. He went through a polished oak double entrance door and passed beneath the archway, which led to a paved courtyard and former stables converted to garages.

The lawyer's gilded plaque was next to the left-hand door and a brass nameplate read:

Maître G. Sabin-Levesque
Lawyer

To the right of the door opposite, a man was watching him through the windows of the concierge's lodge.

Maigret's morning visitor had told him that her apartment was on the first floor. Another brass nameplate bore the words:

Professor Arthur Rollin
Paediatrician
3rd floor
By appointment only

He must be an expensive specialist. The lift was vast. Since he was only going up one floor, Maigret chose the inviting stairs covered in soft carpeting.

On the first floor, he rang the bell. Almost immediately, the door was opened by an amiable young maid who took his hat.

'If you would care to come inside, madame is expecting you . . .'

He found himself in a hallway which was covered with wood panelling, like the large drawing room he was shown into where portraits of figures dating from the first Empire to around 1900 hung on the walls.

He did not sit down. The furniture was heavy, mostly

Louis-Philippe style, and while the overall effect was one of opulence and comfort, there was no joyfulness.

'Madame is waiting for you in her boudoir. I'll show you the way . . .'

They walked through two or three rooms which Maigret didn't have the time to take in, and finally came to a little sitting room with walls covered in blue silk, where the mistress of the house lay on a chaise longue. She was wearing a dressing gown of a darker blue than the walls, and she extended a ring-laden hand. He wondered whether he should shake it or kiss it, and he eventually brushed it with his fingertips.

'Do please sit down. Forgive me for receiving you like this, but I am not feeling well and I think I'll go back to bed after our conversation.'

'I'll try not to keep you for long.'

'What do you think of me?'

'As I said this morning, that you are a very clever woman.'

'In which you are mistaken. I merely follow my instincts.'

'First of all, may I ask you a question? Before coming to report your husband's disappearance to me, did you ask the chief clerk whether he'd heard from him?'

'I telephoned him several times during the past month . . . There's a direct line from the apartment to the office . . . I should tell you that this building, which used to belong to my father-in-law, is now owned by my husband . . .'

'And Monsieur Lecureur . . . that's his name, isn't it? . . . Monsieur Lecureur hasn't heard from him either?'

'Nothing.'

'Did he on previous occasions?'

'I didn't ask him. I believe I told you that we're not on very good terms.'

She hesitated.

'Can I offer you a brandy or would you prefer something else?'

'No. Thank you.'

'I'll have a brandy, myself . . . You see I'm not ashamed to drink in front of you . . . Besides, everyone will tell you I'm an alcoholic, and it's true . . . They might also tell you I'm mad . . .'

She pressed a bell and a few moments later a manservant appeared.

'Honoré, bring me the brandy and a glass.'

'Just one, madame?'

'Just one, yes. Detective Chief Inspector Maigret doesn't feel the need to drink . . .'

There was something aggressive in this new attitude. She was defying him and her wry mouth formed the ghost of a smile.

'Did you and your husband sleep in the same bedroom?'

'We did for three months or so, immediately after our marriage. On this side of the main drawing room, you are in my half of the apartment. The other side is my husband's territory.'

'Do you usually eat together?'

'You have already asked me that . . . Occasionally, but we don't keep the same hours and we don't have the same tastes.'

'What do you do for the holidays?'

'We have . . . sorry . . . Gérard inherited a large villa above Cannes. That's where we go . . . Recently he bought himself a speedboat and I see him even less than in Paris . . .'

'Do you know if he has any enemies?'

'No one as far as I'm aware . . . Except me . . .'

'Do you hate him?'

'I wouldn't say that. I don't bear him a grudge either. That's his nature.'

'Are you his sole heir?'

'The only one, yes.'

'Does he have a large fortune?'

'One which might tempt a lot of women in my situation. But it so happens, you see, that I am not interested in money and I'd be happier in a sixth-floor garret . . .'

'Why don't you ask for a divorce?'

'Out of laziness. Or indifference. There comes a point when you no longer want anything, where each day you go through the same motions without thinking . . .'

She picked up her glass with a trembling hand.

'To your health . . .'

She drained it in one gulp.

'You see? Apparently I should be ashamed . . .'

'Is that what your husband tells you?'

'When I started drinking, yes. That was years and years ago . . .'

'And now?'

'He doesn't care.'

'How would you feel if you were to find out he was dead? Would it be a release?'

'Not really. His existence matters so little to me!'

'Do you think something bad has happened to him?'

'It occurred to me and that's why I came to see you.'

'What could have happened to him?'

'He was in the habit of meeting his . . . let's call them girlfriends . . . in nightclubs where you come across all sorts of people . . .'

'Are you familiar with some of these nightclubs?'

'Two or three. I found matchbooks with the names on . . .'

'For example?'

'Le Chat Botté . . . La Belle Hélène . . . Hold on . . . Le Cric-Crac . . .'

'You were never tempted to see them for yourself?'

'I'm not curious . . .'

'Evidently . . .'

She poured herself a drink and her lips quivered again; her gaze had become cloudy, absent. Maigret had the impression that she would suddenly become aware of his presence and ask him what he was doing there.

'In other words, you're thinking he's been murdered.'

'What about you?'

'Why not taken ill?'

'He has an iron constitution.'

'An accident . . .'

'I'd have read about it in the newspapers . . .'

'Have you telephoned the hospitals?'

'Yesterday.'

And so, despite appearances, she had all her wits about her. On the marble mantelpiece, there was a photograph in a silver frame. Maigret stood up to inspect it more closely. It was Madame Sabin-Levesque, much younger, unmarried most probably, in a studied pose. In those days she was very pretty, with a gamine look.

'That was me, yes . . . I've changed, haven't I?'

'Was this photo taken before or after your marriage?'

'A few weeks after. Gérard insisted I had my portrait taken by a famous photographer in Boulevard Haussmann . . .'

'So he was in love?'

'I don't know. He seemed to be.'

'Did things deteriorate suddenly?'

'No. The first time he ran off for twenty-four hours and I didn't say anything. He told me he'd been to visit a client in another town . . . Then he began to disappear when he felt like it. He stopped informing me. He'd go out after dinner, and I never had any idea when he'd be back . . .'

'What was he like when he was with those who knew him well?'

'They'll all say that he was a happy-go-lucky fellow, who got along with everyone and who was always ready to help people. Some would say there was something childlike about him . . .'

'What about you?'

'I have nothing to complain about. Apparently I misjudged things, or he was wrong about me . . .'

'Meaning?'

'That he thought I was different from what I am . . .'

'What did you do before you met him?'

'I was a legal secretary to Maître Bernard d'Argens, Rue de Rivoli . . . The two men knew each other . . . Gérard came to my boss's office several times and one day he asked me out.'

'Were you born in Paris?'

'No. In Quimper . . .'

'Why do you think he's been killed?'

'Because it's the only explanation.'

'Is your mother still alive?'

'Yes. My father – his name was Louis Frassier – is dead. He was an accountant. My mother was born Countess Outchevka . . .'

'Do you send her money?'

'Of course. Money has never meant anything to Gérard. He would give me anything I wanted without asking any questions . . .'

She drained her glass and raised a handkerchief to her lips.

'May I have your permission to see the rest of the apartment?'

'I'll show you around.'

She rose from the chaise longue and walked towards the door, treading gingerly.

2.

The place gave the impression of great wealth, evoking the prominent, austere families of the nineteenth century. The apartment occupied the entire floor and Madame Sabin-Levesque, still unsteady on her feet, began by showing Maigret the part that was hers.

Beyond the boudoir, there was a very spacious bedroom, the walls of which were also covered in blue silk, which appeared to be her favourite colour. The bed was unmade but she wasn't bothered by this intrusion into her privacy. The furniture was white. There was a bottle of brandy on the chest of drawers.

'What is your first name?' asked Maigret.

'Nathalie. Probably a nod to my Russian background . . .'

The bathroom floor and walls were tiled in blue-grey marble, and, like the bedroom, it was untidy.

Then came a room lined with cupboards, followed by what could be called a small sitting room, a second boudoir.

'This is where I take my meals when I don't eat in the dining room.'

She had the detached air of a museum guide.

'Now, we're entering the servants' quarters.'

A vast room, first of all, with display cabinets full of silverware, then a small dining room painted white, and lastly the kitchen with an old-fashioned stove and copper pans. An old woman was bustling about.

'Marie Jalon, who was already here in my father-in-law's day.'

'When did he die?'

'Ten years ago.'

'So you lived here with him?'

'For five years . . .'

'Did the pair of you get along well?'

'He had no interest in me whatsoever. At that time, I used to eat in the dining room and I can count on one hand the number of times he spoke to me.'

'What kind of relationship did he have with his son?'

'Gérard would go downstairs at nine o'clock. He had an office to himself. I don't know what he did there, exactly.'

'Was he already in the habit of disappearing?'

'For two or three days, yes.'

'And his father didn't say anything?'

'He pretended not to notice . . .'

Maigret was discovering a whole world, an outmoded, inward-looking world.

Perhaps, in the late nineteenth or early twentieth century, there had been receptions and balls in the two drawing rooms. Because there were two and the second one was almost as vast as the first.

Everywhere the walls were covered in wood panelling that had become dark in colour.

Everywhere too were paintings from another era, portraits of men with side whiskers, their necks encased in high collars.

It was as if life had come to a standstill.

'Now, we're entering my husband's side . . .'

A study, with leather-bound books up to the ceiling. A walnut stepladder to reach the top shelves. On the desk, in a corner by the window, lay a blotter and brown leather accessories. Perfectly tidy. There was no indication that a person lived there.

'Is this where he sits in the evenings?'

'When he's at home.'

'I see he has a television.'

'So do I, but I never watch it.'

'Do you ever spend the evening in this room?'

'I did in the early days of our marriage.'

She was struggling to find her words, letting them drop as if they were of no importance. The corners of her mouth were turned down, giving her face a bitter expression.

'His bedroom . . .'

Maigret had had the time to verify that the desk drawers were locked. What could be in them?

There were very high ceilings throughout the apartment, with very tall windows too, their crimson velvet curtains making the rooms gloomy.

The bedroom walls were covered not in wood panelling but in fauve leather. The bed was a double bed. There were armchairs with slightly sagging seats.

'Did you sleep here?'

'Sometimes, during the first three months . . .'

Was that hatred in her voice, written on her face?

She carried on with the guided tour, still as if in a museum.

'His bathroom . . .'

His toothbrush, razor, hairbrush and comb were all still there.

'He never took anything with him?'

'Not as far as I know.'

A dressing room, as in Nathalie's side of the apartment, then a gym.

'Did he use it?'

'Rarely. He'd grown plumper; not exactly fat, but bloated . . .'

She pushed open a door.

'The library . . .'

Thousands of books, from all periods, but with very few recent works.

'Did he read a lot?'

'I didn't come to see what he did in the evenings. This staircase leads directly down to the office, because we've passed over the arch. Do you still need me?'

'I shall probably need to see you again. If so, I'll telephone you.'

She was going to go back to her bottle.

'I presume you'll pay a visit to the office now?'

'Yes, I would like to question Monsieur Lecureur. I apologize for inconveniencing you . . .'

She walked off, arousing in Maigret a mixture of pity and annoyance. He took the stairs, filling a pipe at last, because he had refrained from smoking in the apartment.

He found himself in a large room where half a dozen typists were tapping away feverishly. They looked up and stared at him in surprise.

'Monsieur Lecureur, please.'

On the shelves were hundreds of green files of the sort found in civil service departments and most lawyers' offices. A short, dark-haired woman invited him to follow her across a room where there was just a long table and a massive, ancient safe.

'This way . . .'

Another room, where a middle-aged man sat on his own, poring over what must have been the general ledger. He shot Maigret an indifferent glance as he went through to the next room where five employees were working.

'Is Monsieur Lecureur alone?'

'Yes, I think so.'

'Would you telephone him and ask if he is free to see Detective Chief Inspector Maigret?'

They stood waiting for a moment, then a padded door opened.

'Do come in . . . I am glad to see you . . .'

Lecureur was younger than Maigret had imagined when told that he had worked with Sabin-Levesque's late father. He couldn't have been fifty. He had dark hair, with a little moustache, and his suit was a deep grey, almost black.

'Please have a seat.'

Wood panelling again. The firm's founder must have had a great fondness for dark wood.

'I assume Madame Sabin-Levesque alerted you?'

The Empire-style furniture here was mahogany.

'I presume you're the person who stands in for your boss when he disappears?'

'That is my job as chief clerk. But there are documents I am not authorized to sign and that creates a problem for me.'

He was a calm man, with that particular quality of those who have to rub shoulders with high society. He wasn't servile, but there was a touch of deference in his attitude.

'When he took off for a few days, did he inform you?'

'No. It was unplanned. Of course, I know nothing of his private life . . . I have to make do with suppositions . . . He would often go out in the evenings, almost every evening, as a matter of fact—'

'One moment. Was he actively involved in the firm's work?'

'He spent most of his days in his office and he received most of the clients in person . . . He didn't appear to be very busy and yet he had more to do than me . . . Especially when it came to wealth management and the sale and purchase of estates and chateaux . . . He was exceptionally good at his job and I'd have been incapable of taking his place . . .'

'Is his office next to yours?'

Lecureur went and opened a door.

'This is it . . . The furniture, as you can see, is of the same style, but there are three additional chairs.'

Perfectly tidy. No dust. The lawyer's office overlooked Boulevard Saint-Germain and you could hear the drone of traffic.

The two men sat down again.

'I gather his absences usually lasted only two or three days . . .'

'More recently, they sometimes lasted a week.'

'Did your boss remain in contact with you?'

'He would nearly always telephone me to find out whether there was any new matter he needed to attend to . . .'

'Do you know where he called from?'

'No.'

'As far as you know, did he have a bachelor pad in Paris?'

'It's a possibility that occurred to me. He never had much cash on him and he paid for almost everything by cheque . . . The stubs went through my hands before being passed on to the accounts department—'

He stopped, frowning.

'I'm not sure I'm authorized to discuss these things. I'm bound by professional confidentiality.'

'Not if he's been murdered, for example . . .'

'Do you seriously believe he has?'

'His wife seems to think so.'

He shrugged as if to suggest that what she said was of little consequence.

'I confess that I thought of that too. It's the first time he's been away for so long and hasn't telephoned me. A week ago, he had a meeting here with one of our most important clients, one of the biggest, if not *the* biggest landowner in France.

'He knew this . . . Despite his absent-minded air and his frivolous appearance, he never forgot anything and he tended to be meticulous in his work . . .'

'What did you do?'

'I postponed the appointment with the excuse that he was in hospital.'

'Why, given your suspicions, did you not inform the police?'

'It was up to his wife to do so, not me . . .'

'I understand she never comes down to the office.'

'That is correct . . . In the past, she came down once or twice, but she didn't stay long . . .'

'Was she made to feel uncomfortable?'

'She wasn't welcomed with open arms. Not even by her husband.'

'Why not?'

He fell silent again, even more embarrassed than before.

'I'm sorry, inspector, but you are putting me in an awkward position. My employer's relationship with his wife is none of my business . . .'

'What if a murder has been committed?'

'That would change everything, of course . . . Here we love Monsieur Gérard . . . That's what I call him, because I knew him when he'd just graduated . . . All the staff appreciate him . . . No one takes the liberty of judging his private life . . .'

'I believe one can't say the same for his wife.'

'It's a little as if she were an outsider. I'm not saying she's mad. But all the same she's a thorn in the flesh.'

'Because she drinks?'

'There's that too.'

'Was your boss unhappy with her?'

'He's never complained. He's gradually made a separate life for himself . . .'

'Earlier you mentioned cheque stubs that went through your hands. I assume he made payments to the women with whom he spent several days . . .'

'I suppose so too, but I don't have any evidence . . . Those cheques weren't made out to a named person but to the bearer . . . There were some for five thousand francs and others for twenty thousand . . .'

'Were there any for the same amount every month?'

'No. That's why I don't think he had a bachelor pad.'

They looked at each other now in silence.

'Some members of staff,' sighed the chief clerk, at last, 'saw him going into nightclubs . . . And then there would nearly always be an absence of a few days . . .'

'You think something bad has happened to him, don't you?'

'I fear so. What about you, inspector?'

'From the little I know so far, I do too . . . Did women sometimes telephone him at his office? I presume all calls go through the switchboard . . .'

'I've questioned the switchboard operator, of course . . . There's no trace of any calls of that nature . . .'

'Which suggests that, when he disappeared, he didn't give his real name . . .'

'There's one detail I think I should mention . . . Two weeks ago I was already beginning to get worried . . . I telephoned Madame Sabin-Levesque to tell her and I advised her to contact the police . . .'

'What did she reply?'

'That there wasn't any reason to worry yet and that she would act when the time was right . . .'

'She didn't ask you up to the apartment or come down to discuss the matter with you?'

'No.'

'I don't have any other questions for you at present. If there's any news, please call me at the Police Judiciaire. Just one thing, though. Do the servants upstairs share the feelings of the office staff concerning Madame Sabin-Levesque?'

'Yes. Especially the cook, Marie Jalon, who's worked for the family for forty years and who knew Monsieur Gérard when he was a child. She hates her with a passion.'

'What about the others?'

'They put up with her, that's all. Except the maid, Claire Marelle, who's devoted to her and undresses her before putting her to bed when she finds her employer lying in a stupor on the floor . . .'

'Thank you.'

'Are you going to open an investigation?'

'With not much to build on. I'll keep you posted.'

Maigret left and went into a café close to the Solférino Métro station. He didn't order a brandy, the thought of which he found repugnant, but a large, chilled beer.

'Do you have a telephone token?'

He shut himself up in the booth and looked for the number of the lawyer Nathalie claimed to have worked for before her marriage, Maître Bernard d'Argens. He wasn't listed in the telephone directory.

Maigret drank his beer and took a taxi, giving the address in Rue de Rivoli.

'Wait for me. I shan't be long.'

He went into the concierge's lodge, which was a sort of

small sitting room. The concierge wasn't a woman but a white-haired man.

'Maître d'Argens, please?'

'He died at least ten years ago.'

'Were you already working here?'

'I've been here for thirty years.'

'Who took over his practice?'

'Not a lawyer but an architect, Monsieur Mage.'

'Did he keep some of the staff on?'

'Monsieur d'Argens only had an elderly secretary who took retirement and went back to her home town.'

'Did you know a Mademoiselle Frassier?'

'A pretty brunette, always restless . . . ? She worked for Maître d'Argens over twenty years ago . . . She only stayed for a year because she didn't like the job, and I don't know what became of her . . .'

Maigret, his brow troubled, returned to his taxi. Admittedly, this was only the start of the investigation, but it did not bode well, with so little to go on. Furthermore, he had to act with discretion, because Monsieur Sabin-Levesque could well reappear at any moment.

The sun had gone down behind the buildings. The air was chilly and Maigret regretted leaving his spring coat at the office.

He had the taxi drop him off at the corner of Quai des Orfèvres and Boulevard du Palais because he felt like another glass of beer.

He was still thinking about Nathalie, the strange Madame Sabin-Levesque, and he had a hunch that she knew a lot more than she was telling him.

Back in his office, he filled one of his pipes and went over to the door into the inspectors' office. Lapointe was typing. Janvier was looking out of the window. Lucas was busy on the phone.

'Janvier . . . Lapointe . . . Come into my office, will you . . .'

Janvier too was gradually becoming more experienced and was developing a paunch.

'Are you free, Janvier?'

'Nothing important at the moment. I've finished with the young car thief . . .'

'Have you got the energy to spend the night outdoors?'

'Why not?'

'Go to Boulevard Saint-Germain as soon as you can and watch number 207a . . . If the woman matching the description I'm about to give you leaves the building, follow her . . . You'd better take a car . . .

'She has dark hair, is fairly tall and very thin, with staring eyes and a nervous twitch . . . If she leaves the building, it will probably be on foot, even though she has a chauffeur and two cars . . . One's a Bentley and the other a Fiat . . .

'Tell Lourtie to relieve you tomorrow morning and pass on the instructions . . .'

'How is she dressed?'

'When she came here, she was wearing a fur coat, mink most likely.'

'All right, chief.'

Janvier went out and Maigret turned to Lapointe.

'What about you? No news?'

Lapointe blushed and stammered, without looking directly at Maigret.

'Yes . . . A phone call . . . A few minutes ago . . .'

'From whom?'

'The woman from this morning.'

'What did she want?'

'First of all she asked if you were here . . . I said no. She sounded completely drunk.

' "So who am I speaking to, then?" she said.

' "Inspector Lapointe."

' "That's not the young pup from earlier who was writing down everything I said?"

' "Yes it is."

' "Well, tell the detective chief inspector from me he can go to hell . . . and the same to you . . ." '

Lapointe added, still embarrassed:

'I could hear what sounded like a struggle.

' "Leave me alone, damn you . . ."

'Someone must have grabbed the phone from her hands, because the line went dead.'

Before leaving the Police Judiciaire, Maigret said to Lapointe:

'I'd like you to come and pick me up from my place with one of the cars, at eleven o'clock . . .'

'Tomorrow morning?'

'Tonight. I fancy sniffing around a few nightclubs.'

Madame Maigret had set aside the herrings, which he loved, and he savoured them as he absently watched the news on the television. From his face, she guessed that the case in hand was no run-of-the-mill investigation and that it was preoccupying him, that he was almost making it a personal mission.

It was true. That day, that mild, clear 21st of March, he had been plunged into a world that was foreign to him; above all he'd found himself faced with a type of woman he had never met before and who disconcerted him.

'Take out a dark suit for me, my best one.'

'What's happening?'

'Lapointe is coming to pick me up at eleven. He and I have to visit a couple of nightclubs.'

'That'll cheer you up, won't it?'

'If I can find answers to my questions . . .'

Ensconced in his armchair, he snoozed in front of the television and, at half past ten, his wife brought him a cup of coffee.

'If you have to stay awake all night . . .'

He lit a pipe first, and then sipped his coffee. For him, coffee and pipe went hand in hand.

He freshened up in the bathroom, then changed, as if his appearance might be of importance. A part of him was still stuck in the days when people dressed up to go to the opera and wore a dinner-jacket to go to a nightclub.

It was five to eleven. He thought he heard a car pulling up. He opened the window and saw, parked at the kerb, one of the little black cars belonging to the Police Judiciaire with a lanky figure at the wheel.

He kissed Madame Maigret and headed for the door, grumpy but deep down very pleased not to be the head of the Police Judiciaire.

'Don't wait up for me, whatever you do.'

'Don't worry. I'm sleepy.'

The air wasn't too cold and the moon was rising over

the chimneys. There were still a lot of windows lit up and some of them were open.

'Where are we going, chief?'

Maigret pulled from his pocket the old envelope on which he'd written down the addresses he'd found in the telephone directory.

'Do you know the Chat Botté?'

'No.'

'It's in Rue du Colisée . . .'

On the Champs-Élysées, they followed the two lanes of cars with their lights on that flowed between the rows of neon signs. A doorman with as many stripes as an general stood outside the nightclub. He greeted them with a military salute and opened the double door for them. They went through a thick red curtain and handed their hats and coats to the cloakroom attendant.

The pianist was idly tinkling on the keys, the guitarist was tuning his instrument and, for the time being, no one was at the double bass.

The room was red. Everything was red – the walls, the ceilings, the upholstery – an orangey red which, over-all, was not aggressive but rather cheerful. The bar, in contrast, was in white stucco and the bartender was drying glasses which he put on the shelves behind him.

The maître d' came over to them without much conviction. Perhaps he'd recognized Maigret? Perhaps the two men didn't look like genuine punters?

Maigret waved him away and headed for the bar. Three women were seated at different tables while, at another, a couple appeared to be arguing. It was too early. Things would only begin to get going around midnight.

'Good evening, gentlemen . . . What would you like to drink?'

The bartender had silver hair and a distinguished appearance. He looked at them with feigned indifference.

'I don't suppose you serve beer?'

'No, Monsieur Maigret.'

'Give us whatever you like . . .'

'Dry Martini?'

'Fine . . .'

One of the women came and sat on a stool at the bar, but the silver-haired bartender discreetly signalled to her and she went back to her table.

After pouring their drinks, he asked:

'Well?'

Maigret smiled.

'I admit,' he said, 'we're not here to have fun. Nor are we here to cause you trouble . . . It's information I'm after . . .'

'If I can be of any help, it will be a pleasure . . .'

A kind of understanding had developed between them. The difficulty, for Maigret, was to describe a man he had never seen.

'Of average height, or rather slightly shorter than average. In his early forties . . . Tubby and already paunchy . . . Fair hair, getting a bit thin, and a chubby face . . . He dresses very tastefully, nearly always in beige tones—'

'Are you looking for him?'

'I'd like to track him down.'

'Has he gone missing?'

'Yes.'

'What offence has he committed?'

'None.'

'That could be Monsieur Charles . . .'

'Does he match the description?'

'More or less . . . Very cheerful, isn't he? . . . Always happy . . . ?'

'I believe so.'

'Don't you know him?'

'No.'

'He comes here every so often and sits at the bar, orders a bottle of champagne . . . Then he looks around the room, examining the hostesses closely, one by one . . . He eventually makes up his mind and has the one he likes brought over to him . . .'

'Does he stay late?'

'That depends . . . Sometimes he leaves with the girl . . . Other times he just discreetly slips her a five-hundred-franc note and leaves . . . Probably to go and look elsewhere . . .'

'How long is it since you last saw him?'

'Quite a while . . . Six weeks, maybe . . . Or even two months . . .'

'When he left with one of the women, would she be off work for several days?'

'Keep your voice down. The boss doesn't like that. And he's over there on the floor . . .'

A man in a dinner-jacket, Italian-looking, with waved hair and a thin moustache. He was watching them from a distance. He too had probably recognized Maigret.

'In theory, the hostesses aren't allowed to leave before closing time . . .'

'I know . . . I am also aware that the rules aren't always enforced . . . Are there any young women here who have gone off with him on occasion?'

'Martine, I think . . . If you want to talk to her, you'd do best to go and sit at her table . . . I'll send over a bottle . . .'

The young woman with loose, shoulder-length hair gazed at them with curiosity.

A few customers had arrived, some with their wives, and the band was playing a blues number.

'Have you ordered drinks?' she asked.

'The bartender ordered for us,' grunted Maigret, thinking of the problem he was going to have with his expenses claim.

'Have you been here before?'

'No.'

'Do you want me to call one of my friends over?'

The boss, standing close to the table, said to her:

'Watch out, Martine. They're police.'

'Is it true?' she asked Maigret.

'It's true.'

'Why do you want to talk to me?'

'Because you have been out with Monsieur Charles.'

'And is there any harm in that?'

She wasn't being defiant. She carried on talking in a sweet, soft voice, and seemed to find the whole thing amusing.

'No. It so happens that Monsieur Charles has been

missing for a month. Since the 18th of February to be precise. Have you seen him since that date?'

'Actually I was surprised that he'd stopped coming and I mentioned it to one of my friends . . .'

'What do you think of him?'

'His name isn't Charles, obviously. He must be some big shot who has to keep his real identity secret when he wants to have a bit of fun. He's very elegant, very meticulous. I told him he had a woman's hands, they were so well manicured—'

'Where did you go with him?'

'I thought he was going to take me to a hotel, but he asked if we could go to my place . . . I have a nice studio apartment on Avenue de la Grande-Armée . . . I don't entertain anyone there . . . Besides, I very rarely agree to go out with a customer . . . People think that's what the hostesses are there for, but it's not true . . .'

The champagne was poured and she raised her glass.

'To Monsieur Charles, because it's thanks to him that you're here. I hope nothing's happened to him . . .'

'We don't know. He's simply gone missing . . .'

'Is it his wife who's worried? She's mad, isn't she?'

'Did he talk to you about her?'

'We spent four days together . . . He was funny, because he insisted on helping me with the cooking and washing-up . . . From time to time, he'd tell me about himself, always quite vaguely . . .'

'I won't ask you who he is . . .'

'A big shot, as you guessed . . .'

'Does he live in Paris?'

'Yes.'

'And I suppose that from time to time he goes off on a little jaunt?'

'Exactly . . . Four, five days, a week . . .'

'I phoned the boss, Monsieur Mazotti, to tell him I was ill, but he probably didn't believe me . . . When I came back to work, he was sulking . . .'

'How long ago was this fling you're talking about?'

'Two months? Perhaps a bit longer . . .'

'Had he never come to Rue du Colisée before?'

'I had occasionally spotted him at the bar . . . But he couldn't have found what he was looking for, because he left alone . . .'

'Did he visit other clubs?'

'He didn't tell me, but I assume he did.'

'Did he have a car?'

'No. We walked to my place arm in arm. He was very cheerful . . .'

'Did he drink a lot?'

'Not what you'd call a lot. Just enough to make him tipsy . . .'

'He didn't mention that he had a bachelor pad in town?'

'Did he?'

'I don't know.'

'No. He wanted to come to my place . . . During those four days, we lived like a pair of old lovers . . . He'd watch me have my bath and get dressed . . . He'd lean on the window-sill when I went out to the shops and, by the time I got back, the table was laid . . .'

'Can you think of anything else that might help me find him?'

'No. I'm thinking . . . We went for a stroll in the Bois de Boulogne, but the sky clouded over and we came home quite quickly . . . He was very—'

She stopped talking abruptly, as if prudish.

'Go on.'

'You'll laugh at me . . . He was very affectionate, full of little attentions, like a man in love . . . When he left, he slipped a cheque into my hand . . . Are you leaving so soon?'

Mazotti, the owner, was waiting for them by the red curtain concealing the door.

'Have you found what you were looking for, inspector?'

'Martine will tell you. Goodnight.'

They were getting a clearer idea of Sabin-Levesque's character, and Maigret had learned more about him than from his wife or from his chief clerk.

'Shall we carry on?' asked Lapointe.

'While we're about it . . . The Belle Hélène, Rue de Castiglione . . .'

This club was more sophisticated in appearance. The decor was entirely in pastel colours, and violins were playing a slow waltz. Here too, Maigret made his way over to the bar, followed by Lapointe. He looked at the bartender and frowned.

'So they've let you out?' he asked.

'I was released early for good behaviour . . .'

He was Maurice Mocco, a Corsican gangster with an extensive criminal record.

'What will you have, inspector? . . . What about you, young man? . . . Is he your son, Monsieur Maigret?'

'One of my inspectors.'

'You're not after me, I hope?'

'No.'

'What are you drinking?'

'Two beers . . .'

'Unfortunately, I don't have any . . .'

'Water . . .'

'Are you serious?'

'Yes. Do you know Monsieur Charles?'

'Which one? There are several. One of them, who's completely bald and must be in his seventies, comes from Bordeaux for business once a week and takes the opportunity to drop in here . . . The other one comes less regularly . . . Quite short, very elegant, very pleasant, always dressed in a light-coloured suit . . .'

'Tubby?'

'You could say he's tubby, yes . . .'

'Has he ever gone off with a hostess?'

'He generally leaves them alone, but once, he noticed one, Leila, who stopped working here a long time ago . . . It was last summer . . . They sat talking at the table in the corner, over there . . . Leila kept shaking her head, but he was insistent . . . When he left, I called her over . . .

' "Who the hell is that man?" she asked me.

' "A very respectable gentleman . . ."

' "He insisted he wanted me to go and spend a few days

in the country with him . . . At an inn . . . Somewhere simple, fresh air . . . You've got to be kidding!"

' "What was he offering you in exchange?"

' "Ten thousand at first . . . When he saw I wasn't interested, he upped it to fifteen and then twenty thousand . . . He couldn't believe I was saying no . . . To the country, no way! With all the crazy people around these days . . ." '

'What became of this Leila?'

'I think she married an engineer from Toulouse . . . She never came back here . . .'

Maigret too was in need of some fresh air, because it was suffocating in those nightclubs and the smell of the women's perfume was making him feel sick. He and Lapointe paced up and down the empty street.

'That old crook Mocco has just given us a valuable piece of information, in any case. Monsieur Charles sometimes took his conquests to the countryside . . .'

'I think I see what you mean.'

'Among these women, there are all sorts . . . I knew one who had a PhD in sociology . . . Some have a lover . . . and those lovers aren't always very reputable . . .'

It was two o'clock in the morning. Maigret was no longer sleepy.

Ten minutes later, they stepped out of the car outside the Cric-Crac, in Rue Clément-Marot. Loud pop music spilled out into the street. The façade was rainbow-coloured, as was the room where couples crammed the dance floor.

The bar, once again. But the owner, a certain Ziffer, young and fair-haired, had already approached Maigret and Lapointe.

'Can I help you, gentlemen?'

Maigret flashed his badge under his nose.

'I'm sorry, inspector . . . I didn't recognize you . . . It's so dark in here . . .'

The room, which wasn't large, was lit only by a slowly revolving mirror ball on the ceiling.

'You won't find any irregularities in my establishment, I assure you . . .'

'Do you know Monsieur Charles?'

The fair-haired Ziffer frowned, as if trying to remember something.

It was the bartender who spoke, a very fat man with bushy eyebrows.

'He always used to sit at the bar . . .'

'When was the last time you saw him?'

'Weeks ago . . .'

'Did you see him on the 18th of February?'

'What day was the 18th?'

'A Tuesday . . .'

'It doesn't ring a bell . . . My last recollection is seeing him at the bar with Zoé . . .'

'Did she go off with him?'

'That's not allowed, inspector,' broke in the owner.

'I know . . . I know . . . Did she go off with him?'

'No. But he wrote something down in a little notebook, most likely an address that Zoé gave him . . .'

'Is she here, this Zoé?'

'She's on the dance floor . . . The platinum blonde with amazing breasts . . .'

'I'll go and fetch her for you,' Ziffer hastily offered.

And Maigret, mopping his forehead, said to the bartender:

'I don't suppose you have any beer . . .'

3.

Zoé had the light blue eyes of an innocent little girl. She gazed with curiosity at the stranger, fluttering her eyelashes, and the owner said:

'This is the famous Detective Chief Inspector Maigret and you can be truthful with him.'

She did not appear to have heard of Maigret and she waited patiently, like a schoolgirl waiting for the teacher's questions.

'Do you know Monsieur Charles?'

'By sight, of course. He comes here every so often.'

'What do you call every so often?'

'Almost every week.'

'Does he always leave with a hostess?'

'Oh no! Hardly ever. He watches us all and occasionally he buys a bottle for one of us.'

'Does he dance?'

'Yes. Very badly.'

'How long is it since you've seen him?'

She looked up at the ceiling, again like a schoolgirl.

'Quite a while . . . The last time, we drank a bottle of champagne together . . .'

'Do you remember the date?'

'Yes . . . It was the 18th of February . . .'

'How can you be certain?'

'Because it was my birthday . . . He even bought me flowers from Joséphine, the old flower-seller who comes in every night . . .'

'Did he ask you to leave with him?'

'Yes . . . I was straight with him and told him I had a boyfriend waiting for me at home and he looked peeved . . . I felt bad for him because he was a sweet man . . .'

'Nothing else happened?'

'I told him that, if he wanted a nice girl, I had a friend who wasn't a hostess but who sometimes entertained men at her place . . . Only respectable people . . . I asked him to excuse me for a moment so I could phone her to see if she was free . . . I got through to Dorine . . . She promised she'd be home . . .'

'So you gave her address to Monsieur Charles?'

'Avenue des Ternes, yes . . .'

'What time was that?'

'Around one o'clock in the morning . . .'

'Did he leave right away?'

'Yes . . .'

'Have you seen Dorine since?'

'I called her that same night, at around three, to find out if everything was going OK . . . She told me that Monsieur Charles hadn't turned up and she was still waiting . . . The next time I saw her, she confirmed that no one had come.'

'What about since then?'

'What do you mean?'

'Have you seen Monsieur Charles again?'

'No. I was even surprised that he'd stayed away from here for so long . . .'

'Thank you, Zoé.'

'Is that all?'

'Yes, for the time being.'

Maigret watched her walk off to her table and the owner came over and inquired:

'Are you satisfied?'

'Fairly satisfied.'

So far, it seemed that young Zoé was the last person to have seen the lawyer. It had been one o'clock in the morning when he had left her to go to Avenue des Ternes, but he'd failed to arrive.

'What now, chief?' Lapointe wanted to know once he was at the wheel of the little car.

'My place . . . I've had enough for tonight and you must be sleepy as well . . .'

'Strange fellow, isn't he?'

'A strange fellow, yes. Either he had a particular taste for nightclub hostesses, or he wanted to avoid complicating his life with regular mistresses . . .'

Once home, Maigret started undressing while Madame Maigret, who was in bed, asked him sweetly:

'Had a good time?'

'I think I might have made a little discovery . . . We'll soon find out if it's of any use . . .'

'Not too tired?'

'No. Wake me up at the usual time . . .'

It took him a while to get to sleep because his mind was racing. His thoughts were still filled with the packed nightclubs and the din.

But, all the same, he was in his office by nine o'clock

the next morning, and the first person he spotted in the inspectors' office was Janvier.

'Come in here . . .'

The sun was a little warmer than the previous day and, since he had a slight headache, he went over to open the window.

'Your night?'

'Quiet. Although there was one strange incident.'

'Tell me . . .'

'I'd parked the car fifty metres from the apartment building . . . I stayed at the wheel, my eyes glued to number 207a . . . A few minutes after eleven p.m. the door opened and I saw a woman come out . . .'

'Madame Sabin-Levesque?'

'Yes. She was holding herself stiffly, as if it was an effort for her to walk straight . . . I let her get a little way ahead and then I started up the engine. She didn't go far . . . Not even two hundred metres . . . She went into a public telephone booth . . .'

Maigret knitted his eyebrows.

'She inserted a coin, but it looked as if she didn't get through because she hung up almost immediately . . . The same with the second coin . . . It wasn't until the third attempt that she began to speak . . . She was on the line for a long time, because twice she had to put in more money . . .'

'It's odd that she didn't telephone from home . . . She must believe her line's being tapped . . .'

'I suppose so . . . When she came out of the phone booth, her coat fell open briefly and I saw that she was in her nightdress . . . She went straight back to 207a, pressed the button and the door opened at once . . . Nothing further until the morning . . . I left instructions with Lourtie, and Bonfils will relieve him around midday . . .'

'Have a wiretap put on that telephone as soon as possible . . .'

Janvier was about to leave the office.

'And the office number too . . . Then go to bed . . .'

'Thanks, chief . . .'

Maigret flicked through the post awaiting him, signed a few forms, and dropped in to update the superintendent on his progress.

'Are you going back there?'

'Yes. I don't think you'll see much of me in the office in the coming days.'

Did the big chief know that Maigret had been offered his job? He made no reference to it, but Maigret had the impression that he was treating him with increased respect.

Lapointe had arrived and was a bit out of sorts. He drove Maigret to Boulevard Saint-Germain.

'Shall I come up with you?'

'Yes. I might need you to take notes.'

'I'll bring my shorthand pad.'

Maigret nearly went into the office on the ground floor but decided to go straight up to the apartment. The young maid, Claire Marelle, opened the door and scowled at him.

'If you want to see Madame, I must tell you right away that she's sleeping . . .'

Ignoring her, Maigret stepped inside the hallway, followed by Lapointe.

'Have a seat,' he said to the young woman, indicating a chair.

'I'm not supposed to sit down here . . .'

'You're supposed to do what I tell you . . .'

She eventually sat on the edge of the leather-upholstered chair.

This was why Maigret was sometimes criticized. A high-ranking police officer should summon witnesses to his office, and, as for the clubs he'd visited the previous night, he should have sent an inspector.

Maigret lit his pipe and Claire Marelle glared at him as if he were committing a crime.

'What time did your employer come home last night?'

'To come home, she'd have had to go out.'

'What time did she go out, if you prefer?'

'I have no idea.'

'Were you asleep?'

'As I said, she didn't go out.'

'Devoted as you are, and given the state she's in almost every night, I am certain you must wait up to put her to bed before going to sleep yourself . . .'

She was quite a pretty girl, but her stubborn attitude didn't suit her. She looked at Maigret with apparent indifference.

'So what?'

'I can tell you that she came home at around half past eleven.'

'She's allowed to go out for some air, isn't she?'

'Weren't you worried when you saw her go out? She was having trouble walking straight . . .'

'Did you see her?'

'One of my inspectors did. And do you know why she went out at that hour?'

'No.'

'To telephone from a public phone booth . . . Who was she in the habit of phoning before these past few days?'

'No one . . . Her hairdresser . . . Shops . . .'

'I'm talking about more private conversations . . . People don't call their hairdresser at eleven o'clock at night, or their bootmaker . . .'

'I don't know anything.'

'Do you feel sorry for her?'

'Yes.'

'Why?'

'Because she was unlucky to land a husband like hers . . . She could be living the life she deserves, be a socialite, go out, entertain friends . . .'

'And her husband stops her from doing so?'

'He doesn't take any notice of her. He sometimes disappears for a whole week, but this time he's been gone for over a month . . .'

'Where do you think he is?'

'With some girl or other . . . He only likes girls he picks up God-knows-where . . .'

'Has he asked you to sleep with him?'

'Just let him try . . .'

'Fine. Go and bring the cook to me and, while I'm talking to her, wake your mistress up and tell her I want to see her in around ten minutes . . .'

She obeyed reluctantly, after giving him a furious look, while Maigret winked at Lapointe.

Marie Jalon, the cook, was short and broad, quite plump, and she stared at Maigret with curiosity, as if thrilled to meet him in the flesh.

'Sit down, madame. I already know that you've been part of the household for a long time . . .'

'Forty years . . . I was here when Monsieur's father was still alive . . .'

'Has anything changed since?'

She gave a deep sigh.

'Everything has changed, my good sir. Since that woman's been here, everything's been topsy-turvy . . . There's no longer any routine . . . Mealtimes are whenever she decides to eat . . . There are days when she has nothing at all and then, in the middle of the night, I hear a noise in the kitchen and I find her rummaging around in the fridge . . .'

'Do you think it upsets your employer?'

'Definitely . . . He doesn't say anything about it . . . I've never heard him complain, but I know he's resigned to it . . . I've known him since he wasn't even ten years old and he was always hanging on to my apron strings . . . He was timid even then . . .'

'So in your view, he is a timid person?'

'I'll say he is! If you knew about the scenes he puts up with, without protest and without daring to raise a hand to her . . .'

'Aren't you worried about his absence?'

'I wasn't at first . . . It's quite usual . . . He has to have his little compensations from time to time.'

Maigret smiled at the expression.

'What I'm wondering is who alerted you . . . Unless it was Monsieur Lecureur . . .'

'No.'

'Was it Madame Sabin-Levesque who came to tell you she was worried?'

'Yes, she spoke to me. As for worried? . . . I can see you don't know her . . . She'd watch him die at her feet without raising her little finger . . .'

'Do you think she's mad?'

'She's an alcoholic, yes . . . She starts drinking before she's even finished her morning coffee . . .'

'Have you not seen your employer since the 18th of February?'

'No.'

'Have you heard from him at all?'

'Nothing . . . I have to admit that I'm really in a state about it . . .'

Madame Sabin-Levesque was standing very still by the drawing room door. She was wearing the same dressing gown as on the previous day and hadn't bothered to run a comb through her hair.

'Have you come to see my cook?'

'Both of you . . .'

'I'm at your disposal . . .'

She showed the two men into the boudoir where she had received them the day before. There was a bottle of brandy and a glass on a silver tray.

'I presume I can't offer you a drink?'

Maigret shook his head.

'What do you want of me this time?'

'To ask you a question, first of all. Where did you go last night?'

'I know from my maid that you've put me under surveillance. That saves me having to lie. I didn't feel well and I went out for some air. On seeing a telephone booth, I had an urge to call one of my friends . . .'

'So you have friends?'

'It may surprise you, but I do . . .'

'Can I ask the name of the woman you called?'

'That's none of your business and I shan't answer.'

'Was this friend of yours not at home?'

'How do you know?'

'You must have phoned three different numbers . . .'

She said nothing but took a sip of brandy. She was not well. She would most likely have felt groggy on waking in the mornings, and alcohol was the only thing that restored her poise to some degree. Her face was puffy and her nose seemed longer and more pointed.

'Another question for you. The drawers in your husband's private desk are locked. Do you know where the keys are?'

'In his pocket, I presume. I haven't searched his rooms.'

'Who was his closest friend?'

'In the early days of our marriage, he often used to invite Auboineau, the lawyer, and his wife to dinner . . . He and my husband were students together . . .'

'Do they still see each other these days?'

'I don't know . . . Be that as it may, Auboineau doesn't

come here any more . . . I didn't like him . . . He's a preten-
tious man who talks non-stop, as if he thinks he's in
court . . . As for his wife—'

'What about his wife?'

'No matter. She's very proud of having inherited her
parents' chateau.'

She had another drink.

'Is this going to take long?'

Maigret could tell she was tired and he felt rather sorry
for her.

'I suppose one of your men is still keeping a watch
on me?'

'Yes. I've finished for this morning . . .'

Maigret signalled to Lapointe to follow him.

'Goodbye, madame.'

She did not reply and the maid was waiting for them in
the drawing room to show them into the hallway and
then out of the door.

On the ground floor, Maigret went through the arch,
walked into the firm's office and asked to speak to Monsieur Lecureur. The latter came out to greet the two police
officers and invited them into his office.

'Do you have any news?' he asked.

'Not news, exactly. As far as I know, the last person who
saw your boss was a hostess at the Cric-Crac in Rue Clément-
Marot, and when he left her he was supposed to go to
Avenue des Ternes, where a young woman was expecting
him . . . That was in the middle of the night of the 18th of
February . . . He never turned up at Avenue des Ternes . . .'

'Perhaps he changed his mind on the way?'

'Perhaps . . . Are you certain that he hasn't telephoned you even once for over a month?'

'Not once.'

'Whereas during his previous absences he remained in telephone contact with you . . .'

'Every two or three days, yes. He was very conscientious. Two years ago, he came rushing back because we needed his signature . . .'

'How were your relations with him?'

'Very cordial . . . He trusted me completely . . .'

'Do you know what he kept in the drawers of his desk upstairs?'

'I have no idea. I seldom went up to the apartment and I've never seen the drawers open . . .'

'Have you seen the keys?'

'Often. He had a set which he always kept on him. Among them was the key to the big safe which you must have noticed in the typing pool.'

'What does it contain?'

'Our clients' confidential papers, especially their wills—'

'Do you also have the key?'

'Of course.'

'Who else does?'

'No one.'

'Were there matters that your boss dealt with in person, without talking to you about them?'

'He saw some clients on his own in his office, almost always took notes and, once they'd left, he put me in the picture.'

'Who was in charge of financial transactions when he was away?'

'Me. I have a power of attorney.'

'Is your boss very wealthy?'

'He's wealthy, yes.'

'Has he increased his fortune since his father died?'

'Most certainly.'

'And his wife is his sole heir?'

'I and another member of staff acted as witnesses when he drew up his will, but I didn't read it. I presume he made provision for a number of fairly large bequests.'

'What about the firm?'

'It will all depend on Madame Sabin-Levesque.'

'Thank you.'

And Maigret suddenly became aware that since Nathalie's visit to the Police Judiciaire, people spoke of the lawyer sometimes in the present and sometimes in the past tense.

Mainly in the past.

'If you wish to see me today, come right away, because I'm operating at one o'clock . . .'

Doctor Florian, it seemed to Maigret, was not averse to a certain formality, like many society doctors. He lived on Avenue Foch, which suggested a select clientele.

'I'll be there in a few minutes . . .'

He and Lapointe were in a bar on Boulevard Saint-Germain, having a beer and making phone calls.

'He's expecting us . . . Avenue Foch . . .'

A few moments later, the little black car was driving up

the Champs-Élysées. Lapointe was silent, slightly down-cast, as if there was something troubling him.

'What's on your mind?'

'It's that woman . . . I can't help feeling sorry for her . . .'

Maigret said nothing, but he must have been thinking the same thing because, as they drove around the Arc de Triomphe, he muttered:

'I'm waiting to get to know her a little better . . .'

The apartment building was luxurious, imposing, more modern than the one on Boulevard Saint-Germain. A spacious lift took them smoothly up to the sixth floor where a manservant in a striped waistcoat opened the door to them.

'This way . . . The professor is expecting you . . .'

First of all, he relieved them of their hats and coats. Then he opened a double door guarded on either side by Greek statues that were almost intact.

The surgeon was taller and broader than Maigret, and he shook his hand vigorously.

'Inspector Lapointe . . .' said Maigret, introducing his colleague.

'I apologize for rushing you, but I have a heavy work-load. For the past fifteen minutes – since your telephone call – I have been wondering how I can help you . . .'

The study was vast, very luxurious, with sunlight streaming in. The French window, which opened on to a terrace, stood ajar and the curtains billowed in the breeze.

'Please have a seat . . .'

His greying hair made him look older than his years

and he was dressed austerely in striped trousers and a black jacket.

'You are a friend of Gérard Sabin-Levesque's, unless I'm mistaken . . .'

'We are the same age and were at university together. He was studying law, while I studied medicine . . . We were part of a boisterous crowd and he was the life and soul . . .'

'Has he changed a great deal?'

'I haven't seen much of him since he got married . . .'

Doctor Florian's expression clouded.

'I have to ask you why you are questioning me like this. As a doctor, I am bound by professional confidentiality, and as a friend, I have a duty to maintain a certain discretion . . .'

'I understand. Sabin-Levesque has been missing for over a month . . . He told no one he was going away, neither his wife nor his chief clerk.

'One evening, on the 18th of February, he walked out of his home without any luggage. I've tracked his movements, that evening, or rather, that night, to a nightclub in Rue Clément-Marot, the Cric-Crac. He left alone, for an address he'd been given on Avenue des Ternes, but he never showed up there . . .'

'What does his wife say?'

'Do you know her?'

'In the early days of their marriage, I saw the two of them quite frequently.'

'Was he already in the habit of what I call absconding?'

'You know about it? Even as a student, he was drawn

to women and to the atmosphere of nightclubs . . . He still is, but there's nothing pathological about it and the word "absconding" is inappropriate, as it happens.'

'I use it for want of anything better . . .'

'He didn't confide in me on that subject during our dinners but I don't think he ever stopped going out as a bachelor, as it were . . .'

'Did you know his wife well?'

'I met her a dozen or so times . . .'

'Did he tell you how they met?'

'He's very secretive about it . . . I don't think she's from the same sort of family as he is . . . I am vaguely aware that at one point in her life she was a secretary, in a law firm, I believe . . .'

'That's correct. What impression did you have of her?'

'She didn't say much to me. During our dinners she seemed dejected, or aggressive, and sometimes she'd leave the table mumbling an excuse . . .'

'Do you think she's of sound mind?'

'That's not my department. I am a surgeon, not a psychiatrist. I think her main problem was that she drank a lot . . .'

'She's drinking more and more. She was inebriated when she came to Quai des Orfèvres to inform me of her husband's disappearance . . .'

'When was that?'

'Two days ago.'

'And he's been missing since February?'

'Yes. She waited over a month. After a week, the chief clerk suggested she speak to the police and she told him to mind his own business . . .'

'That's strange.'

'Worrying, more than anything.'

The doctor lit a cigarette with a gold lighter and said to Maigret:

'You may smoke your pipe . . . Your questions are troubling. What I can tell you is that Gérard was, and must still be, a very brilliant man. When I met him, he was already a playboy, as it's called these days. He loved sports cars and places where people have fun. He rarely turned up to lectures, I was told, but he still managed to sail through his exams.

'I don't know whether he's changed . . .'

'That's how people have described him to me. He appears to have married on impulse and very soon realized his mistake . . .'

'That's what I think too . . . It's because of his wife that he's found himself socially isolated . . . Nathalie would humiliate him in front of his friends . . . I never heard him respond . . . He would carry on the conversation as if no one had spoken . . .'

'Then he lived with her as if she didn't exist . . . Do you think that was painful for him?'

'It is hard to judge when someone's always joking . . . Clearly he wasn't living a normal life . . . I understand the little escapades he indulged in . . . The fact that he's been missing for a month is more serious . . . Has he not even been in touch with his office?'

'Even though he was in the habit of calling in. This time, he didn't bother to check whether he was needed . . .'

'You seem very concerned about his wife . . .'

'She lived in the same apartment and there was probably a time when they spoke of love . . .'

'Poor old Gérard . . .'

The doctor rose to his feet.

'Forgive me, but I must get back to work . . . By the way, we have a mutual friend who became a psychiatrist and is based at Sainte-Anne . . . Doctor Amadieu, who lives in the Latin Quarter . . . You'll find his address in the phone book . . . He was also a guest at several of the Sabin-Levesques' dinners . . .'

He showed them to the door where the manservant was waiting with their coats over his arm.

'Ten past twelve . . .' said Maigret once they were back in the little car. 'The main thing is to find out whether Doctor Amadieu goes home for lunch . . .'

Which gave him an excuse to have an aperitif, in order to telephone. This time, he chose a pastis without hesitating.

'The same for me,' muttered Lapointe.

Amadieu was home. He didn't resume work until two o'clock.

'I presume it's urgent?'

'I believe the case I'd like to discuss with you is urgent, yes.'

Amadieu lived in an apartment amid a certain degree of untidiness, and he appeared to be single, because there was only one place setting at the table, which the maid was clearing away. He had thick, auburn hair and freckles, and his tweed suit was as crumpled as if he'd slept in it.

Maigret would subsequently learn that he was one of

the most renowned psychiatrists in France, if not in Europe.

'Have a seat. Smoke your pipe and tell me what you'd like to drink.'

'Nothing for now. I know your time is precious. You knew Sabin-Levesque very well . . .'

'In our student days, we went on enough jaunts together for me to know him . . . Don't tell me he's in trouble with the police . . . ?'

'He hasn't been in touch with anyone for over a month . . .'

'No one?'

'No one. Since he left, he hasn't even telephoned his chief clerk as he always did when he went off for less than a week . . .'

'What can have happened to him?' said Amadieu to himself.

Then, as if surprised:

'And how do you think I can help you?'

'I'm looking for a man I have never seen and about whom yesterday I knew absolutely nothing, and I need to build up some idea of him.'

'I see.'

'Your friend Florian, from whose place I've just come and who gave me your name, considers him to be a strong character.'

'So do I.'

'Could the life he's been living for such a long time have pushed him to commit suicide?'

'He's not the type. Besides, he found his compensations . . .'

'I know. I've met several of his girlfriends . . .'

'After he got married, I went to dinner at Boulevard Saint-Germain several times . . .'

'Merely as a friend?'

'I think I can answer that question without betraying professional confidentiality . . . It was Gérard who asked me to come and observe his wife . . . He wondered whether she was mentally sound . . . I discovered a woman with a sharp mind who, from the first evening, saw right through me . . . She looked at me calmly, as if she was defying me . . . She deliberately drank non-stop . . .'

'She still does . . .'

'I know but, when I was there, she drank twice as much and, each time she refilled her glass, she would glance at me.

' "It's an illness, isn't it, doctor?" she'd say. "I'm what's called an incurable alcoholic . . ."

' "People can be cured of almost anything, madame, so long as they want to be cured, of course . . ."

' "How can a person want it if they can't face up to life . . . I'm here, alone, despised by a husband who doesn't have the slightest affection for me . . ."

' "I am certain you are mistaken. I know Gérard. If he married you, it's because he loved you . . ."

' "He thought he loved me . . . I didn't love him, but I hoped I would learn to . . . He's the most selfish, cynical person I've ever come across . . ." '

Amadieu relit his pipe and blew a puff of smoke up towards the ceiling. There were books and journals scattered all around the room, which was neither a sitting room nor a study, nor a consulting room.

'You see the situation in which I found myself. Poor Gérard, who was present, put up with it without batting an eyelid.

'On my sixth or seventh visit, she made her way over to me, in the big drawing room, before I'd had a chance to greet her, and she said in a slurred voice:

' "Monsieur Amadieu, don't bother to come any further. There won't be any dinner and from now on you will not be welcome in this house. When I need a psychiatrist, I'll choose one for myself . . ."

'She turned her back on me and stumbled in the direction of her rooms.

'The next day, my friend Gérard turned up here to apologize. He told me that she was becoming more and more insufferable and that he was doing everything he possibly could to avoid her. Admittedly, he added that she was doing likewise . . .'

'Why didn't your friend ask for a divorce?'

'Because, despite the life he leads, he is a fervent Catholic. And besides, his behaviour would count against him.'

Maigret smoked and gazed pensively at the burly redhead with Delft-blue eyes. At length, he rose and sighed:

'So you don't think she's mad after all?'

'Not at first sight. Don't forget that I only saw her under the influence of drink. It would take more extensive and thorough observations to reach a diagnosis . . . I'm sorry I can't be of more help . . .'

They shook hands and Amadieu watched the two men go down the stairs because there was no lift.

'Brasserie Dauphine?'

'Gladly, chief.'

'A pity we can't send her to Sainte-Anne under the care of a man like that . . .'

'Her husband must find it unbearable at times to live with her, even if they avoid each other. Knowing that she's under the same roof. Given her feelings towards him, I think I'd be afraid . . .'

Maigret looked at Lapointe solemnly.

'Do you think she'd be capable . . . ?'

'I said earlier that I felt sorry for her . . . I still do, because she must be very unhappy, but at the same time, she scares me . . .'

'In any case, he's out there somewhere, dead or alive . . .'

'Dead, most likely . . .' sighed Lapointe very quietly.

The first thing Maigret did on walking into the Brasserie Dauphine, was to head for the telephone and request his home number.

'I know,' said Madame Maigret before he could open his mouth. 'You won't be home for lunch. I was so certain that I haven't cooked anything and you'd have had to make do with ham and salad.'

He was tempted to order a second pastis, but he remembered his friend Pardon's advice and refrained from having an aperitif. On the menu there was tripe *à la mode de Caen*, which he was also supposed to avoid, but which he relished anyway.

'I'm loath to ask the public prosecutor for a search warrant. I'd have difficulty obtaining one, given that there's no proof that a murder has been committed . . .'

'What would you look for?'

'A weapon . . . Did Savin-Levesque have a revolver? . . . Does his wife have one . . . ?'

'But do you think her capable of killing him?'

'I think anything is possible as far as she's concerned. She could just as well have killed him with a poker or a bottle . . .'

'And what would she have done with the body?'

'I know. I can't exactly see her waiting for her husband to come out of the Cric-Crac, knocking him out, since there were no shots, and disposing of the body . . .'

'Maybe she has an accomplice?'

'Unless we're barking up the wrong tree and our man was attacked by thugs . . . People are mugged in the street every night . . .'

'Why, in that case, go to the trouble of getting rid of the body?'

'I know . . . I know . . . I'm going round in circles . . . There are moments when I think I'm getting close to the answer and a second later I realize that it doesn't make sense . . .'

He gave a forced little laugh.

'The best thing would be if our lawyer were to reappear suddenly, bright and breezy, and ask what was wrong with us . . .'

'What do you think of Lecureur?'

'The chief clerk? I don't like him very much, for no

particular reason. He's one of those cold men who are unflappable and who remain composed in all circumstances . . .'

'You spoke about what would happen to the firm if it turns out that Sabin-Levesque is dead . . . Lecureur's been working there for over twenty years . . . He must be tempted to consider the business almost as his own . . .'

'The widow will have to agree to keep him on, which I think is unlikely . . . There doesn't seem to be much love lost between them . . .'

'It's not as if they would kiss in front of us . . .'

Maigret gave Lapointe a long, hard look.

'Do you really think so?'

'Since this morning, yes . . . I could be wrong but . . .'

'That would be too easy, wouldn't it? The pair of them are very clever. Nathalie is really wild . . . You heard what the psychiatrist told us . . . It reminds me of a phrase I read recently: *Frenzied to the point of losing consciousness* . . .'

'Do you reckon that could apply to her?'

'Yes. When she's been drinking, at any rate . . . And the way she is, under the influence of alcohol from the moment she wakes up, that makes her a dangerous woman . . .'

'But to go so far as killing her husband . . .'

'I know . . . And yet, she gets carried away . . . I'll go back and see her, just to push her into a corner . . .'

'Supposing she's the one who was afraid?'

'Of whom?'

'Of her husband . . . He might sometimes want her dead . . .

'He's put up with her for over fifteen years, true, but there's a point when something snaps . . .'

Maigret gave a wry laugh.

'Look at the pair of us, building theories on the basis of suppositions . . .'

He didn't have a brandy after his coffee. He was going to be put off brandy for a long time after seeing Madame Sabin-Levesque knock it back like water.

4.

Maigret was seated at his desk staring glassily at the man sitting opposite him, who was dressed in a chauffeur's strict livery and awkwardly turning his cap over and over in his hands.

Lapointe and his trusty shorthand notepad were at the back of the office. It was Lapointe who had gone to fetch the chauffeur from Boulevard Saint-Germain and he'd found him in his room above the garages.

Maigret had had to urge the nervous man to sit down.

'Vittorio Petrini?'

'Yes, monsieur.'

He was so well trained that he looked as though he might stand to attention at any moment.

'You were born . . . ?'

'In Patino, a small village south of Naples.'

'Are you married?'

'No, monsieur.'

'How long have you been in France?'

'Ten years, monsieur.'

'Did you start working for your current employers straight away?'

'No, monsieur. I was with the Marquis d'Orcel for four years.'

'Why did you leave?'

'Because he died, monsieur.'

'Tell me what your duties consist of at the Sabin-Levesques'.'

'I don't have a lot of work, monsieur. In the morning, I do the shopping for Mademoiselle Jalon—'

'The cook?'

'She has difficulty walking. She's quite elderly. Then I'd maintain the cars, unless monsieur needed me.'

'You're speaking in the past tense . . .'

'I beg your pardon, monsieur?'

'You are speaking as if that was in the past.'

'I haven't seen monsieur for a long time.'

'Which car did he use?'

'Sometimes the Fiat, sometimes the Bentley, it depended on which clients he was going to see. We would sometimes travel fifty, even a hundred kilometres from Paris. A lot of Monsieur's clients are very old and don't come into the city any more. Some of them live in very fine chateaux—'

'Did your boss chat to you while you drove?'

'Sometimes, monsieur. He's a very good boss, not proud, nearly always in a good mood.'

'Does Madame ever go out in the morning?'

'Almost never. Claire, her maid, told me she gets up very late. Sometimes she doesn't have lunch.'

'What about in the afternoons?'

'Monsieur almost never needed me. He stayed at the office.'

'He didn't drive himself?'

'Sometimes, but he preferred to take the Fiat . . .'

'What about Madame?'

'She would sometimes go out at around four or five o'clock. Without me. Without a car. Apparently she went to the cinema, nearly always to one of the cinemas in the Latin Quarter, and came home by taxi.'

'Did it not strike you as odd that she didn't ask you to drive her there or pick her up?'

'Yes, monsieur. But it's not my place to judge.'

'Would she sometimes ask you to drive her?'

'Once or twice a week.'

'Where would she usually go?'

'Not far. Rue de Ponthieu. To a little English bar where she'd stay for quite some time.'

'Do you know the name of the bar?'

'Yes, monsieur. The Pickwick . . .'

'What state would she be in when she came out?'

The chauffeur was reluctant to reply.

'Drunk?' insisted Maigret.

'Sometimes I'd help her into the car.'

'Would she go straight home?'

'Not always. Every so often she'd ask me to stop outside another bar, the one in the George V hotel.'

'Did she come out of there alone too?'

'Yes, monsieur.'

'Was she able to get into the car?'

'I'd help her, monsieur.'

'What about the evenings?'

'She never went out in the evenings.'

'And your boss?'

'He'd go out, but without a car. I think he preferred to take taxis.'

'Every evening?'

'Oh! No. He'd sometimes not go out for eight or ten days.'

'And did he sometimes not come home for several days?'

'Yes, monsieur.'

'Did you ever drive them anywhere together?'

'Never, monsieur. Or rather only once, for a funeral. Three or four years ago . . .'

He was still fiddling with his peaked cap with its leather visor. His blue uniform was well tailored, his shoes gleaming.

'What do you think of Madame?'

He was embarrassed and gave the ghost of a smile.

'Don't you know? It's not my place to talk about her . . . I'm only the chauffeur . . .'

'How did she behave with you?'

'It varied. Sometimes, she didn't say a word and was tight-lipped as if she was angry with me. At other times she called me her little Vito and chatted non-stop . . .'

'About what?'

'It's hard to say. For instance:

' "I wonder how I can put up with this life a moment longer . . ."

'Or, when she told me to drive her home:

' "To the jailhouse, Vito . . ." '

'Was that what she called the apartment on Boulevard Saint-Germain?'

'When she'd been to several bars, yes.

' "You know it's because of my pig of a husband that I drink. Any wife would do the same in my shoes . . ." '

'That sort of thing, you see . . . I'd listen in silence. I am very fond of Monsieur . . .'

'What about her?'

'I'd prefer not to answer.'

'Do you remember the 18th of February?'

'No, monsieur.'

'It's the day your boss left the apartment for the last time.'

'He must have gone out alone, because he didn't ask for a car.'

'How do you spend your evenings?'

'I read, or I watch television. I'm trying to lose my accent, but it's difficult—'

The telephone rang, interrupting their conversation. Maigret signalled to Lapointe to answer it.

'Yes . . . He's here . . . I'll put him on . . .'

And to Maigret:

'It's the chief inspector of the fifteenth arrondissement . . .'

'Hello, Jadot . . .'

Maigret knew him well and liked him a lot.

'I'm sorry to bother you, Maigret . . . I thought that what I have to say might be of particular interest to you . . . A Belgian bargeman, Jef van Roeten, who was testing his engine at Quai de Grenelle, was surprised to see a body float up to the surface in the wash—'

'Have you identified it?'

'The wallet was still in the trouser pocket . . . Gérard Sabin-Levesque, does that ring a bell?'

'Yes, damn it. Are you at the scene?'

'Not yet. I wanted to let you know first of all. Who is he?'

'A lawyer from Boulevard Saint-Germain who's been missing for over a month. I'm on my way. I'll meet you there . . . And thank you . . .'

Maigret stuffed a second pipe in his pocket and turned to the chauffeur.

'I don't need you any more for the time being. You may go. I appreciate your cooperation . . .'

As soon as he was alone with Lapointe, Maigret said:

'He's dead all right . . .'

'Sabin-Levesque?'

'His body has just been fished out of the Seine, at Quai de Grenelle . . . Come with me . . . Inform Criminal Records first . . .'

The little car weaved in and out of the traffic and reached Pont de Grenelle in record time. Below the road, on the quayside, were planks, piles of bricks and barrels. Two or three barges were unloading.

Some fifty people had gathered around an inert form, and a police officer was struggling to hold the crowd back.

Jadot was already there.

'The deputy public prosecutor will be here shortly . . .'

'Do you have the wallet?'

'Yes . . .'

He handed it over to Maigret. Naturally it was soft, squidgy and soaked through. It contained three 500-franc and a few 100-franc notes, an identity card and a driving licence. The ink had run but some words were still legible.

'Nothing else?'

'Yes. A cheque book . . .'

'Again in Sabin-Levesque's name?'

'Yes.'

Maigret glanced furtively at the sodden form lying on the ground. He had to steel himself to go closer, as always in these cases.

The bloated stomach was like an overfilled goatskin. The chest was gaping and ugly white viscera spilled out. As for the face, there was almost nothing human left.

'Lapointe, telephone Lecureur and tell him to come right away . . .'

He couldn't impose such a sight on Nathalie.

'Where is the bargeman?'

A voice with a strong Belgian accent replied:

'I'm here, monsieur . . .'

'How long have you been moored at this spot?'

'More than two weeks, you see. I was planning to stay only two days to unload my bricks, but my engine packed up. Some mechanics came to repair it. It took a while. They finished this morning . . .'

His flaxen-haired wife, with a blond baby in her arms, was next to him, but she appeared not to understand French and her eyes flitted anxiously from one of them to the other.

'At around three o'clock, I wanted to try out the engine myself, because I plan to leave for Belgium tomorrow morning after loading up with wine at Bercy . . . I noticed some resistance and, when the engine started up, this here body suddenly rose up to the surface . . . It must have been caught on the anchor or the propeller, which explains why it's all mangled . . . Just my luck, isn't it, monsieur . . .'

The deputy public prosecutor, who was no more than

thirty, was called Oron. He was very dapper, very distinguished.

'Who is he?' he asked, after shaking Maigret's hand.

'A man who's been missing for over a month, Sabin-Levesque, a lawyer from Boulevard Saint-Germain . . .'

'Did he run off with the takings?'

'It appears not.'

'Did he have any reason to kill himself?'

'I don't think so. The last person to have seen him alive was a nightclub hostess . . .'

'Might he have been murdered?'

'It's likely.'

'Here?'

'I don't see how he could have been brought alive to the banks of the Seine. He was no fool . . . Hello, Grenier . . . I've got an unpleasant job for you . . .'

'So I see . . .'

He was one of the new forensic pathologists.

'I can't do anything here. It would be absurd for me to certify the death, because it is pretty obvious . . .'

A van from the Forensic Institute pulled up, but first of all they had to allow the photographers from Criminal Records to do their job. The lawyer's chief clerk arrived shortly afterwards and descended the stone steps to the loading dock.

Maigret pointed to the shapeless heap giving off a fetid smell.

'See if it is definitely him . . .'

The chief clerk was loath to approach. He was rigid and held his handkerchief over his nose and mouth.

85

'It's definitely him,' he announced.

'How can you recognize him?'

'By his face. It might be horribly disfigured, but it's definitely him. Do you think he threw himself into the water?'

'Why would he have done that?'

Lecureur stepped back, keeping as far away from the body as possible.

'I don't know. A lot of people throw themselves into the water . . .'

'I have his wallet and chequebook . . .'

'So I identified him correctly . . .'

'I'll summon you to Quai des Orfèvres tomorrow morning to sign your statement . . .'

'At what time?'

'Nine o'clock . . . Do you have a taxi waiting?'

'Vito was just back . . . I asked him to drive me here . . . He's up there on the road with the Fiat . . .'

'In that case, I'll hop in too . . . Are you coming, Lapointe?'

He went over to the pathologist, the only person not to seem upset by the body.

'Will you be able to let me know by this evening whether he was murdered before being thrown into the river?'

'I'll do my best . . . Given the condition he's in, that won't be easy . . .'

The three men strode through the crowd of onlookers. Jef van Roeten ran after Maigret.

'You're in charge, aren't you?'

'Yes.'

'Can I leave tomorrow morning? I've told you everything I know . . .'

'First of all, you're going to come to the police station to sign a written statement.'

'Which police station?'

'That gentleman over there with a black overcoat and a little moustache is the chief inspector of the local police station and he'll tell you what you have to do . . .'

There were four of them in the little Fiat, which Vito, like all private chauffeurs, drove smoothly.

'Excuse me, Monsieur Maigret,' muttered the chief clerk. 'Could we stop for a minute at a bar? If I don't have a strong drink, I might be sick . . .'

The three of them got out at a bar where there were only two dock workers. Lecureur, whey-faced, ordered a double brandy. Maigret contented himself with a beer but Lapointe also had a brandy.

'I wasn't expecting him to be found in the Seine.'

'Why not?'

'I don't know. I imagined that he'd gone off with a woman . . . He could have been on the Riviera, anywhere . . . The only thing that made me think something had happened to him was that he didn't telephone me . . .'

They soon reached Boulevard Saint-Germain.

'Go over all the recent accounts and find out from the bank—'

'Will you give me the cheque book so that I can check the amounts on the stubs?'

Maigret handed it to him and headed for the door on

the right, while the chief clerk went through the one on the left.

'You again!' exclaimed the maid in annoyance on opening the door.

'Yes, mademoiselle, it's me again. And I'd be obliged if you'd tell your mistress right away that I am waiting for her.'

He made his own way to the boudoir and, as if in defiance, kept his pipe in his mouth.

Ten minutes or so went by and, when Nathalie appeared, she was not in a dressing gown but was wearing a very elegant suit.

'I was about to go out.'

'To which bar?'

'That's none of your business.'

'I have some important news for you. Your husband has been found . . .'

She didn't query whether he was dead or alive.

'Where?' was all she asked.

'In the Seine, under Pont de Grenelle . . .'

'I was certain something had happened to him . . .'

The corners of her mouth were turned down, her gaze quite steadfast. She had been drinking, for sure, but she held firm.

'I presume I have to go and identify the body? Is he at the mortuary?'

'First of all, the mortuary was abolished ages ago. Now it's called the Forensic Institute.'

'Will you be driving me there?'

'There's no need for you to identify him. Monsieur Lecureur took charge of it. But, if you insist—'

'Is that an insult?'

'How?'

'You believe I have such morbid desires?'

'One never knows, with you . . .'

The sacrosanct bottle of brandy was on the pedestal table with some glasses. She poured herself a drink, without offering her visitors anything.

'What's going to happen now?'

'By this evening, the press will know and reporters and photographers will be ringing your doorbell.'

'Is there no way of stopping them?'

'You can refuse to speak to them.'

'Then what?'

'Then they'll go sniffing around somewhere else. They won't go easy on you, quite the opposite. They're a prickly lot. They might find out about certain things—'

'I have nothing to hide.'

'Do as you wish, but in your shoes, I'd see them. I'd try to be as presentable as possible. The first ones will be here in an hour at the most.'

She drank a second glass nonetheless.

'They're in touch with the police stations . . .'

'You enjoy speaking to me like this, don't you?'

'Believe me, I don't.'

'You hate me . . .'

'I don't hate anyone . . .'

'Is that all you had to say to me?'

'That's all, yes. We'll see each other again very soon, no doubt.'

'I have no wish to see you. I despise you, Monsieur

Maigret. And now, get out of here . . . Claire! . . . Throw these people out . . .'

There was still a police officer on the pavement opposite 207a, and Maigret was in two minds whether to stop the surveillance, but in the end he decided to continue with it. The telephone tap had been fruitless, as he should have expected because Nathalie had had no hesitation in going outside at night to call from a public phone booth, wearing a nightdress beneath her fur coat.

'What do you think, Lapointe?' asked Maigret as he clambered into the car.

'If she behaves like that with the reporters, she can expect some hostile press coverage tomorrow morning . . .'

'I don't have anything more to do at the office today, so drop me off at home . . .'

Madame Maigret greeted him with a mischievous smile.

'Happy?'

'Why should I be happy?'

'You've found your body, haven't you?'

'The radio?'

'Yes, there was a brief mention on the six o'clock news . . . Are you hungry?'

'No. Not after the few hours I've just spent.'

He went over to the cupboard and wondered what to have to drink, because he was feeling queasy. In the end he poured himself a small glass of gin, which was rare. The bottle had been there for more than a year.

'Do you want some?' he asked.

'No, thank you . . . Sit down for a few minutes and read the papers and I'll rustle up a light meal.'

The soup was already made. She then served a ham salad with cold potatoes.

'You're worried, aren't you?' she said quietly while they were eating.

'There are things I don't understand, and I don't like that.'

'Who are you working with?'

She was aware that he always teamed up with one of his closest colleagues. Sometimes it was Janvier, sometimes Lucas, but these days it was Lucas who stood in for him when he was away. On this case, he happened to be working with Lapointe.

'Shall I turn the television on?'

'No. I'm feeling too lazy to watch it.'

He settled in his armchair and went back to skimming the newspapers, his mind elsewhere, mainly on Nathalie, who had just thrown him out of her apartment and spoken so rudely.

By nine o'clock, Maigret had dozed off and his wife was about to wake him up so that he could go to bed when the telephone rang, making him jump.

'Hello . . . Yes, speaking . . . Is that you, Grenier? . . . Did you find out anything?'

'First of all, a question. Was this gentleman in the habit of wearing a hat?'

Maigret thought for a moment.

'I have never seen him and it didn't occur to me to question his wife or his employees on the subject . . . Wait . . .

He dressed elegantly, in a very youthful style . . . I imagine him bareheaded . . .'

'Otherwise someone removed his hat before hitting him over the head . . . Not just once, in my view, but a dozen times, very violently . . . His skull is in pieces, like a jigsaw puzzle . . .'

'No bullets?'

'Not in his head or anywhere else . . . I don't know what weapon the murderer used: a hammer, a spanner, or a tyre iron . . . Most likely a tyre iron . . . Two blows would have been sufficient to kill him, but the murderer was in a frenzy . . .'

'What about that sort of hole by his waist?'

'That's more recent. The body was partially decomposed when it got caught on an anchor or something like that . . .

'There's one detail I find interesting . . . His ankles were badly damaged by what looks like wire to me, so much so that one of his feet has almost been cut off . . . That wire must have been used to tie the body to a weight, a breeze block or some heavy object . . .'

'How long do you think he'd been in the water?'

'It's hard to be precise . . . Several weeks . . .'

'Four or five weeks?'

'It's possible. By the way, I examined his clothes. In one of the pockets, I found a set of keys . . . I'll send them over to you first thing tomorrow morning . . .'

'I'm eager to see them.'

'You have more people than I do. You could send someone to fetch them.'

'All right. Leave them with the concierge.'

'I'm now going to have a nice hot bath and treat myself to a good dinner . . . I wouldn't like to have to do this kind of work every day . . . Goodnight, Maigret.'

'Goodnight, Grenier . . . And thank you.'

The following morning, Maigret was in his office before nine. His first task was to send an inspector to pick up the keys from the Forensic Institute.

There was a knock on his door. It was Lapointe, who immediately grasped that there was a new development.

'Grenier telephoned me . . . Sabin-Levesque was knocked unconscious with a blunt instrument, as they say in reports. A dozen extremely violent blows . . . The murderer tied a rock or a weight of some sort to his ankles before throwing him into the water . . .

'Lastly, Grenier found a set of keys in one of his pockets . . .'

'Have you seen the papers?'

'Not yet.'

Lapointe went to fetch them from the inspectors' office and brought them to Maigret with a strange smile on his face.

'Look . . .'

One of the daily newspapers bore the headline:

RENOWNED LAWYER MURDERED

The photograph was quite unexpected for someone who had seen Nathalie perhaps an hour before it was taken. There wasn't the slightest trace of her drunkenness.

93

She had made the effort to get changed, and wore a black suit and white lace blouse in place of her beige suit.

Her brown hair was carefully styled. The expression on her face, which looked more elongated, was sad, a photogenic sadness, and she was holding a handkerchief as if she'd just been crying and was afraid of breaking down again.

HIS GRIEF-STRICKEN WIDOW IS BAFFLED

The interview with Nathalie was quite lengthy. She had received the journalist not in the boudoir but in the big drawing room.

'When did your husband go missing?'

'About a month ago. I wasn't worried because he would sometimes have to go and see one of his clients in the provinces.'

'Who is replacing him at the firm?'

'His chief clerk, who is very competent. My husband trusted him fully and had given him power of attorney.'

'Did the two of you go out a lot?'

'Rarely. We only entertained our few friends occasionally. We led a quiet life.'

'Was it you who went to the police?'

'I decided to go and see Detective Chief Inspector Maigret to tell him of my concerns.'

'Why Maigret?'

'I don't know . . . I'd read about several of his cases and felt I could trust him . . .'

There was a shorter interview with Jean Lecureur.

'I have nothing to say.'
'Didn't he leave you a message?'
'No. He never left me messages, but he would telephone me every two or three days . . .'
'Did he do so this time?'
'No.'
'Were you not worried?'
'After around ten days . . .'
'Did it not occur to you to go to the police?'
'I merely informed Madame Sabin-Levesque of my fears.'

Another newspaper published a photo of Nathalie, seated, in the big drawing room.

MYSTERIOUS DEATH OF PARIS LAWYER

The article was more or less the same, except that this newspaper emphasized the fact that the police hadn't been informed. It ended with:

It would seem that Monsieur Sabin-Levesque was in the habit of mysteriously disappearing.

'The amazing thing,' said Lapointe with admiration in his voice, 'is the way she transformed herself in such a short time.'
The inspector came back with the set of keys, which

comprised half a dozen small keys and the key to a safe, probably the one on the ground floor.

Bonfils brought him the list of Paris nightclubs and cabarets and Maigret was surprised at how many there were. The list filled three pages, single spaced.

He slipped it into his drawer, stood up and sighed:

'Boulevard Saint-Germain . . .'

'Do you think she'll see you?'

'She's not the person I want to see. But first of all, I have to go up to the prosecutor's office . . .'

He learned that the examining magistrate in charge of the case was Coindet, a genial and good-natured elderly judge. Maigret had known him since the early days of his career. He found his office at the far end of the examining magistrates' corridor.

Coindet held out his hand.

'I was expecting you. Have a seat.'

The clerk was typing and was about the same age as Coindet.

'I only know what I've read in the papers, since I haven't received a report yet.'

'Because there's nothing to report,' replied Maigret returning his smile. 'The body was only found yesterday, remember.'

'I've heard that you have been investigating for three days.'

'In vain. I need a search warrant, for this morning.'

'Boulevard Saint-Germain?'

'Yes. Madame Sabin-Levesque has taken a dislike to me . . .'

'That doesn't come across in her interview . . .'

'She tells the press what she wants them to hear . . . I want to search the lawyer's apartment from top to bottom. Until now I've only been able to have a quick look around.'

'You won't leave me too long without an update?'

This was an allusion to Maigret's reputation. He was famed for carrying out his investigations as he saw fit, without paying any attention to the examining magistrates.

Twenty minutes later, he and Lapointe walked under the arch they were beginning to know well. It occurred to Maigret to go into the lodge, where he was greeted by a very dignified male concierge. The lodge was like a living room.

'I was wondering whether you'd come and talk to me, inspector . . .'

'I've been so busy . . .'

'I understand. I'm a former police officer; I used to work in Traffic . . . I presume you're intrigued by the lady?'

'You don't come across her sort every day.'

'They certainly are – or were, since the man is dead – a strange couple. Here are people who have two cars and a chauffeur. But when they go out, it's usually on foot. I've never seen them leave together and I've heard they take their meals separately.'

'Nearly always.'

'They don't entertain, despite what she told the journalists. The husband goes off from time to time, his head in the clouds and his hands in his pockets like a young man, not taking anything with him. I presume he has a second household somewhere or a bachelor pad in town . . .'

'I'll come back and see you if I need to. You seem very observant.'

'Habit, isn't it?'

A few moments later, Maigret rang the Sabin-Levesques' bell.

Claire flushed with anger on seeing the two men and she would probably have slammed the door in their faces if Maigret hadn't taken the precaution of wedging his foot in the doorway.

'Madame is—'

'I'm not interested in Madame. If you can read, read this document. It's a search warrant, issued by the examining magistrate. Unless you'd like to be arrested for obstructing the course of justice . . .'

'What do you want to see?'

'I don't need you. I know my way around . . .'

And, followed by Lapointe, he headed for the lawyer's rooms. He was particularly interested in the desk. Of all the pieces of furniture, the little mahogany desk was the only one whose four drawers were locked.

'Open the window, would you? It smells musty in here . . .'

He tried three keys before finding the right one. The drawer contained only letter-headed paper, envelopes and two fountain-pens, one of solid gold.

The contents of the second drawer were more interesting. There were a number of photographs, mostly taken on the Riviera, in the grounds of an enormous 1900s-style villa. Nathalie was some twenty years younger and the lawyer, in his shirt-sleeves, looked like a student.

On the back was written 'La Florentine', which was clearly the name of the villa.

In one of the photos, a big Alsatian stood very close to Sabin-Levesque.

It suddenly dawned on Maigret that there was neither a dog nor a cat in the apartment.

He was about to shut the drawer when, right at the back, he spotted a little passport photo of the kind that comes from an automatic booth. It was Nathalie, even younger than in the Cannes photos, and more importantly, very different. Her smile was deliberately mysterious, her eyes questioning.

On the back, a single word – a name: Trika.

It was obviously an alias and she hadn't chosen it to work as a lawyer's secretary in Rue de Rivoli.

When she'd told Maigret about her past and given him the name of her supposed former employer, and above all when he'd learned that the latter had been dead for ten years, it had set Maigret thinking.

At that point, she knew that her husband was dead and there was no one to contradict her. She had probably never been a secretary, or even a shorthand typist.

'Look, Lapointe . . . What does she remind you of?'

Lapointe thought for a moment.

'A high-class hooker . . .'

'And we know where Sabin-Levesque went to look for his female companions.'

Maigret carefully slid the photo into his wallet. Then he opened the left-hand drawers. The top one contained unused cheque books. But there was one that had no cheques left and the stubs, instead of having the name of the payee written on them, all said 'Pay bearer'.

There were other odds and ends: a wristwatch, cuff-links, each set with a little yellow stone, elastic bands, stamps.

'Are you enjoying yourself?'

She was there, of course. Claire had dragged her out of bed. He could tell she'd just drunk a large slug of brandy because she reeked of alcohol from a metre away.

'Hello, Trika . . .'

She had enough self-control not to recoil.

'I don't understand.'

'It doesn't matter. Read this . . .'

He held out the search warrant, which she brushed aside.

'I know. My maid told me. So make yourselves at home. Do you want to search my dressing gown?'

Her eyes were different from the previous day. They expressed more than anxiety – a terror which she could barely disguise. Her lips were trembling more than ever, and so were her hands.

'I'm not done with this apartment yet.'

'Does my presence bother you? . . . I haven't had the occasion to set foot in these rooms for a very long time . . .'

Ignoring her, Maigret opened and shut doors and drawers, and went into the closet, sliding back the doors.

He found some thirty suits, mostly in light colours. They bore the label of one of Paris' most renowned tailors.

'It appears your husband didn't wear a hat . . .'

'Since I never went out with him, I wouldn't know . . .'

'Congratulations on your performance yesterday with the press . . .'

Despite her state of mind, she was flattered and couldn't help smiling.

The bed was vast and low, the room very masculine with its leather-covered walls.

The bathroom looked as if it had been used the previous day. The toothbrush was in its place, in a glass, the razor on a stand, with the shaving soap and an alum stone. The floor and walls were of white marble, as were the bathtub and other fittings. There was a picture window with a view over a garden which Maigret was seeing for the first time.

'Is that your garden?' he asked.

'Why wouldn't it be?'

It was rare to find such beautiful trees in a private garden in Paris.

'By the way, Trika, in which club were you a hostess?'

'I know my rights. I'm not obliged to answer you.'

'But you will have to answer the examining magistrate.'

'In that case, I'll have my lawyer with me.'

'Because you already have a lawyer?'

'I've had one for a very long time.'

'The one on Rue de Rivoli?' he asked sardonically.

He wasn't being harsh with her deliberately. But her behaviour tended to exasperate him.

'That's my business.'

'Now let's go into your apartment . . .'

In passing, he read a few of the titles of the books on

the shelves in the study. There were contemporary authors, all distinguished names, and a number of books in English, which the lawyer must have spoken fluently.

After crossing the small sitting room and the drawing room, they ended up in Nathalie's boudoir. She stood there gazing at them. Maigret opened a few drawers, which contained nothing but trinkets of no interest.

He went into her bedroom. The bed was as big as Sabin-Levesque's, but it was white, as was the rest of the furniture. The drawers mainly contained very fine underwear, most likely custom-made.

The grey-blue marble bathroom was in a mess, as if it had just been used in haste. The bottle of brandy and a glass were still on one of the shelves.

Dresses, coats and suits in the closet and, on special shelving, thirty or forty pairs of shoes.

'Do you know how your husband died?'

Her mouth set tight, she looked at him without answering.

'He was hit over the head with a heavy object, most likely a tyre iron. He wasn't hit once but a dozen times, and his skull was literally fractured into tiny pieces.'

She didn't move a muscle. She stood there frozen, gazing at Maigret, and at that moment, anyone would have taken her for a madwoman.

5.

Maigret stopped at the concierge's lodge.

'Tell me, when he got married, Sabin-Levesque had a dog, didn't he?'

'A beautiful Alsatian, which he adored, and the dog loved him too.'

'Did it die?'

'No. A few days after they got back from Cannes, where they spent their honeymoon, they gave it away . . .'

'Did you find that strange?'

'Apparently the dog snarled every time Madame Sabin-Levesque went near it. Once, it even made to bite her and ripped the hem of her dress. She was very scared of it. She made her husband get rid of the animal.'

Once in his office, Maigret sent for the photographer from Criminal Records. First, he showed him the photo of the couple, in Cannes, with the dog.

'Can you enlarge this print?'

'The result won't be brilliant, but the people will be recognizable . . .'

'What about this one?'

It was the passport photo.

'I'll do my best. When do you want them for?'

'Tomorrow morning . . .'

The photographer sighed. With Maigret, everything was always urgent. He was long used to it.

Madame Maigret glanced anxiously at her husband as she always did when he was conducting a difficult investigation. She wasn't surprised by his silence or by his ill-humour. It was as though, once home, he didn't know what to do with himself.

He ate absent-mindedly and his wife would ask with a smile:

'Are you here?'

Because his mind was elsewhere. She remembered a conversation between the two men, one evening when they'd been having dinner at Doctor Pardon's.

'There's one thing,' Pardon had said, 'that I find hard to understand. You're the exact opposite of a law enforcer. One might even say, when you arrest a wrongdoer, that you are sorry.'

'Yes, that is sometimes true.'

'And yet you take your investigations to heart as if you are personally involved . . .'

And Maigret had merely replied:

'Because each time I am caught up in a human experience. When you're called out to the bedside of an unknown patient, don't you feel personally involved too? Don't you fight against death as if the patient were someone dear to you?'

He was tired and dejected. Admittedly, the sight of the body at the Grenelle docks was enough to turn the stomach even of a forensic pathologist.

Maigret had grown fond of Sabin-Levesque, even though he'd never met him. He'd had a friend, at school, who had a similar character. Outwardly he was light-hearted and carefree. In class, he was the most disruptive pupil, interrupting the teacher or doodling in the margins of his exercise books.

When he was sent out of the classroom for an hour, he would press his nose to the window and make funny faces.

But the teachers didn't hold it against him, and they ended up laughing. Admittedly, in the exams, he was always in the top three.

The lawyer, who once led a playboy existence, had suddenly married. Why? Had he fallen head over heels in love? Had Nathalie, who called herself Trika, operated with extraordinary cunning?

What had she been hoping for? A society life, a luxurious apartment, travel, visits to fashionable resorts?

A moment had come, after around three months of conjugal life, when Sabin-Levesque had started going out again.

Why?

Maigret asked himself the question and couldn't find a satisfactory answer. Had she gradually shown herself as she was now? Peace had ceased to reign and, later, they would no longer speak to each other.

Neither of them had requested a divorce.

Maigret ended up dropping off, his head full of question marks. When he got up, after drinking the first cup of coffee his wife brought him in bed, a fine drizzle was falling outside.

'Have you got a busy day ahead?'

'I don't know. I never know what's in store for me.'

He took a taxi. That was a sign. He usually took the bus or the Métro.

The photographs were waiting on his desk and they were unexpectedly clear. He took one of each and headed for Peretti's office, at the other end of the corridor. Peretti was head of the Vice Squad and was the only chief inspector to wear a gold ring set with a yellow diamond, as if the people he mingled with in the line of duty had rubbed off on him.

He was a good-looking man, still young, with very black hair and a flamboyant taste in clothes.

'Well, hello! I haven't seen you for a long time.'

It was true. Their offices were on the same corridor, but their paths rarely crossed. When they did it was mainly at the Brasserie Dauphine.

'I don't suppose you recognize this person?'

Peretti examined the enlarged portrait of Nathalie and went over to the window to see it in the light.

'Isn't that the wife of the lawyer whose photo was in the papers yesterday, when she was younger?'

'That's her, a little over fifteen years ago . . . Here she is with her husband, a few weeks or a few months later . . .'

Peretti studied the Cannes photo just as closely.

'Neither of them rings any bells . . .'

'As I expected. But that's not all. I had my men draw up a list of all the nightclubs in Paris. Here's a copy. Are there any that still have the same owner as in those days? I'm particularly interested in the eighth arrondissement and around there.'

Peretti looked at the list.

'Most of these clubs didn't exist fifteen years ago. Fashions change. There was a period when Montmartre was the centre of night life. Then there was Saint-Germain-des-Prés . . .

'Hold on . . . The Ciel de Lit, Rue de Ponthieu . . . It was and still is run by a charming scoundrel who's never been in trouble with the law . . .'

'Any others?'

'Chez Mademoiselle, Avenue de la Grande-Armée. A very stylish place, owned by a woman, Blanche Bonnard. She must be over fifty, but she's in good shape. She has another club in Montmartre, Rue Fontaine, a less classy joint: the Doux Frisson . . .'

'Do you know where she lives?'

'Her apartment is on Avenue de Wagram and I've heard she spent a small fortune on it . . .'

'I'll leave the list with you, I have other copies. If by chance something occurs to you . . .

'I forgot to ask where the owner of the Ciel de Lit lives . . .'

'Marcel Lenoir? In the same building as his club, on the third or fourth floor. I've had to search his place for drugs . . .'

'Thanks.'

'Your investigation?'

'So-so . . .'

Maigret went back to his office. He attended the morning briefing as usual, and, looking at the superintendent in his chair, he said to himself that he could have been sitting there in a month's time.

'This lawyer business, Maigret?'

The other divisional chiefs were there, each with their case files.

'I haven't made any headway. I'm gathering information which may or may never be useful . . .'

He had the enlarged photo of Nathalie sent to the newspapers, with the caption: 'Madame Sabin-Levesque, at the age of twenty'.

Then he went up to Records to find out whether there was a file under her name or under that of Trika. There was nothing. She didn't have a criminal record and she'd never been arrested for any reason.

'Will you drive me to Rue de Ponthieu?'

It was Lapointe who chauffeured him around, or Janvier, because Maigret had never sat at the wheel of a car. He had bought one recently, so they could get to their little house in Meung-sur Loire on Saturday evenings or Sunday mornings, but Madame Maigret was the one who drove.

'Anything new, chief?'

'We're going to see the owner of a nightclub. He's been running it for over twenty years.'

The club's shutters were closed, but outside were photos of semi-naked women in a large frame.

They walked in through the main entrance. The concierge sent them up to the third floor, left-hand apartment. A little maid of dubious cleanliness opened the door.

'Monsieur Lenoir? . . . I don't know if he can see you now . . . He's just got up and is in the middle of his breakfast . . .'

'Tell him it's Detective Chief Inspector Maigret . . .'

A moment later, Lenoir came to greet his visitors in the passage. He was enormous, very fat, and he wasn't exactly a spring chicken. He was wearing an old burgundy dressing gown over faded pyjamas.

'To what do I owe the honour—?'

'It's not a question of honour. Carry on eating . . .'

'I'm sorry to receive you like this . . .'

Lenoir was an old rogue who, twenty-five years earlier, had run a brothel. He must be around sixty now, but unshaven, his eyes still sleepy, he looked older.

'Please come this way . . .'

The apartment was as ill-kempt as its occupant and there was a mess everywhere. They went into a little dining room whose window overlooked the street.

One soft-boiled egg had been shelled, and Lenoir sliced the top off a second.

'In the mornings, I need to put myself to rights . . .'

He drank black coffee and there were cigarette butts in the ashtray.

'So, what do you say?'

'I'd like to show you a photo and ask you if it reminds you of anything . . .'

He held out the enlarged portrait of Nathalie.

'I know that face from somewhere . . . What's her name?'

'At that time, around fifteen years ago, she called herself Trika . . .'

'They all choose the most ridiculous pseudonyms . . . Trika . . .'

'Do you recognize her?'

'No, to be honest . . .'

'Might you be able to find her name in your books?'

Lenoir ate messily and had egg yolk on his chin and on his dressing-gown lapel.

'Do you think I keep a register with the names of all the girls who pass through my club? . . . These women come and go . . . A lot of them get married and people would be surprised to learn how many do very well for themselves . . . I had one who became a duchess, in England . . .'

'Do you not keep their photographs either?'

'They nearly all ask for them back when they leave . . . The others I tear up and throw away . . .'

'Thank you, Lenoir.'

'My pleasure . . .'

He stood up, his mouth full, and showed them out to the landing.

'31, Avenue de Wagram . . .'

It was an elegant building, home to, among others, two doctors, a dentist and a financial adviser.

'Who shall I say is asking?' inquired the servant girl, dressed like a stage maid.

'Maigret.'

'The detective?'

'Yes.'

Blanche Bonnard wasn't having her breakfast but was on the telephone. Her voice could be heard coming from one of the rooms:

'Yes . . . Yes . . . My dear, I can't commit just like that . . . I need more detailed information and a report from my architect . . . Yes . . . No, I don't know how long that'll take me . . . Will I see you tonight at the club? . . . As you wish . . . Bye . . .'

She came to greet them and her footsteps were muffled by the carpet scattered with brightly coloured rugs. She gazed steadily at Maigret and glanced only briefly at Lapointe.

'You're lucky I'm up and about. I'm normally a late riser, but today I have an appointment with my business adviser . . . Come . . .'

The sitting room was plush, too plush for Maigret's taste. Like Lenoir, the woman must have been over fifty, but she still looked good, even in her casual morning wear. She was fat but agreeably well-proportioned, and she had very beautiful eyes.

'The Sabin-Levesque case, I suppose? I was expecting you sooner or later but I didn't think you'd be so quick . . .'

She lit a gilt-tipped cigarette.

'You may smoke . . . It doesn't even bother my parrot . . . When I saw the photograph in the papers yesterday, it gave me a jolt, and I checked to make sure I wasn't mistaken . . .'

'Did you know Madame Sabin-Levesque when she went by the name of Trika?'

'Did I know her!'

She got up and went into another room, and returned with a huge album.

'Seeing as I don't have a very good memory, I keep everything. I have five albums like this, filled with photos . . . Here . . .'

She handed the open album to Maigret. On the right-hand page there was one of those typical nightclub portraits.

It was definitely Nathalie, still very young, looking innocent and spontaneous. She wore a very low-cut dress that revealed her cleavage.

Beside her, leaning over slightly, was Sabin-Levesque . . . On the table, a champagne bucket and a bottle.

'This is where he met her . . . She'd been a hostess for around two months—'

'Do you know where she came from?'

'Yes. From Nice, where she'd worked in a fairly seedy club.'

'Did she confide in you?'

'They all confide in me. Most of them are lonely, with no one they can talk to . . . So they turn to Mama Blanche . . . Can I offer you something? . . . I don't drink much, but it's time for my port.'

It was port of excellent quality, the likes of which Maigret had rarely tasted.

'Her surname was Frassier and her father died when she was fifteen. He was a book-keeper or something like that . . . Her mother was the daughter of a Russian count, and she liked everyone to know it . . . You see, I do remember things after all . . .

'In my club, she always sat at the same table. The clients were intimidated by her youth and innocence. They were quite tentative in approaching her. She smiled sweetly at them but remained aloof . . .

'She rarely went out with anyone. I don't think it happened more than three times . . .'

'Did she have a regular lover?'

'No. She lived alone in a little hotel room not far from here, in Rue Brey. I was fond of her, but at the same time I couldn't completely understand her . . .

'One evening, Gérard Sabin-Levesque came in . . . or rather Monsieur Charles, which is the name we all knew him by . . . He'd been before, a long time previously . . . He liked gentle, quiet women and he noticed Trika right away . . . He went over and sat down at her table . . . I imagine he asked her to go off with him and she said no . . .

'He returned every night for more than a week, before he managed to persuade her to leave with him. She left some things here. Two dresses, underwear, little personal knick-knacks . . .

'After a few days, she came back to collect her belongings.

' "The love of your life?" I asked her.

'She looked at me without answering.

' "Has he set you up with a place?"

' "There's nothing definite yet . . ."

'She kissed me on both cheeks and thanked me, and that was the last I saw of her.

'Two months later, though, a wedding photo was published in *Le Figaro*. Trika wore a wedding dress, and her husband was in tails.

'*This morning, Monsieur Gérard Sabin-Levesque, the renowned lawyer of Boulevard Saint-Germain, married . . .*'

Maigret and Lapointe exchanged looks. What were they to make of this story? The little girl from Quimper, the hostess in a dubious club in Nice, and then at Chez

Mademoiselle, had become the wife of one of the best-known and wealthiest lawyers in Paris.

Gérard's father was still alive at the time, a man of principles. What had he said about this union? And had the three people who lived on the same floor got on together?

After three months, Gérard had already gone back to his old habit of occasionally disappearing for a few days.

Had Nathalie started drinking then? And did she spend most of her time in her apartment?

The years passed and she drank more and more. The lawyer had given up on the idea of married life. They'd become strangers to each other, if not enemies.

'And now she's free . . . Free and wealthy . . . That niggles you, doesn't it, inspector?'

'The papers didn't tell the full story. Sabin-Levesque received at least ten blows to the head from a heavy object and his skull is in smithereens . . .'

'Do you think a woman could have done that?'

'There are times when women can be as strong as men, if not stronger . . . Supposing she were guilty, where would the murder have been committed? . . . In their apartment? . . . He lost a lot of blood . . . There'd be bloodstains, and she's clever enough to know it . . .

'And besides, how would she have transported the body to the Seine? How would she have got him downstairs to the car and put him inside?'

'Of course . . . The killer could be some thug who attacked him in an empty street.'

'His wallet is untouched and contained over fifteen hundred francs.'

'Revenge?'

'By whom?'

'A lover? . . . The lover of one of the women he picked up in a nightclub . . . ?'

'Those people aren't jealous of paying customers . . . At worst one of them would have attempted to blackmail him . . .'

Maigret glanced again at the photograph of the young couple with the bottle of champagne in front of them and drained his glass of port.

'Another?'

'No thank you, excellent as it is . . .'

He had learned a number of things about Nathalie's past, but where was it all leading him?

He went home for lunch and Madame Maigret was surprised, but it had no significance. Her husband was still as withdrawn, still as grumpy.

He barely noticed what he was eating, even though he usually adored her *pot-au-feu* served with poor-man's sauce.

'A large cup of coffee . . .'

That meant his morning cup, which held a good third of a litre. He skimmed the papers featuring interviews with the concierge and one of the law firm's employees. Vito had also been questioned, but he had given only evasive replies.

On arrival at his office, Maigret found the phone-tapping report.

Nathalie hadn't made a single call since her line had been

tapped, but she had received an extremely brief one that same morning.

'Is that you?'

'Yes.'

'I have to see you . . .'

She had hung up at once, without saying anything. On the same line but from a different telephone, most likely, the cook had called the butcher to order a veal roast which Vito would collect later.

The office, on the other hand, had received an avalanche of telephone calls from anxious clients. Lecureur tried to reassure them and gave them the information they requested.

Maigret went up to see the examining magistrate, but in all honesty, he had little news for him. Good old Coindet wasn't in any hurry. Sitting at his desk, he was slowly puffing away on an old pipe and flicking through a file.

'Take a seat, Maigret.'

'I have almost nothing to tell you. I expect you've received the autopsy report . . .'

'Yes, this morning . . . The murderer won't be able to claim that he had no intention of killing . . . You have no idea where the crime was committed?'

'So far, no . . . The forensic experts from Criminal Records are studying every seam of his clothing and his shoes. Given the amount of time the body was in the water, there's not much chance of obtaining any results . . .'

Maigret passed his tobacco pouch to the magistrate and lit the pipe he'd just filled.

'There's only one area in which I've made some progress.

Madame Sabin-Levesque claimed that, when she met her future husband, she was secretary to a lawyer in Rue de Rivoli. But that lawyer has been dead for ten years, so he can't contradict her.

'In one of the dead man's drawers, which contained a number of photographs, I came across a snapshot of Nathalie when she was much younger, and there was a name on the back: Trika.

'A pseudonym, obviously. Knowing Sabin-Levesque's tastes, I went looking around the nightclubs and I learned that she'd been a hostess, not a secretary. I even found out where she met Sabin-Levesque . . .'

The magistrate sat there, looking pensive, his gaze following the smoke from his pipe.

'Did she ever return to those places?' he asked quietly.

'No, not as far as I know . . . Once she became Madame Sabin-Levesque, she must have had nothing but contempt for that scene, where she felt humiliated . . .

'This morning, she received a telephone call. It was a man's voice, but we didn't have time to locate the caller. The man said:

' "I have to see you . . ."

'She hung up without a word. I have the feeling that she knows a lot more than she's letting on. That's why I'm subjecting her to a sort of harassment. I'm going to see her again, without any particular reason.'

The two men smoked for a while in silence, then they shook hands and Maigret went back to his office.

Walking into the adjacent room, he asked Janvier:

'Who's on duty at Boulevard Saint-Germain?'

'Inspector Baron . . .'

Turning to Lapointe, who was waiting for a signal, Maigret muttered:

'I'm going there on my own . . . It's an experiment . . . She'll be less intimidated and perhaps . . .'

He didn't finish his sentence but gave a dismissive gesture that meant that he didn't have high hopes.

He took a taxi which dropped him off opposite the building. A man was pacing up and down on the other side of the boulevard and Maigret went up to him.

'Has she come out?'

'No. Nothing to report. Only the chauffeur drove out this morning in the Fiat and I presume he was going to the shops because he was back soon afterwards . . .'

The concierge was such a decent man, had been so proud to shake Maigret's hand, that the latter dropped in to say hello.

'Apparently she hasn't left the building?'

'No. The people who came in were all for the doctor on the third floor.'

'How long have you worked here?'

'Sixteen years. I have sensitive feet and being on traffic duty was no good for me.'

'When you started, was Sabin-Levesque still a bachelor?'

'He got married six months after I arrived.'

'Did he still sometimes go off for several days at a time?'

'Except the last two or three weeks before the wedding.'

'Was that while his father was still alive?'

'Yes. A fine figure of a man, every inch the lawyer. He had a young face, but his hair was completely white.'

'Did he get on well with his son?'

'I don't think he was all that proud of him, but he was resigned . . .'

Maigret went up to the first floor and rang the bell.

Claire, the maid, opened the door and gave him a scornful look.

'Madame Sabin-Levesque has gone out.'

'Are you certain?'

'Yes.'

'What time did she leave?'

'At around two o'clock . . .'

It was now ten past three.

'Did she take one of the cars?'

'I don't think so.'

Maigret knew Baron well enough to be certain that nothing could distract him from his task of watching the building. The concierge too would have seen Nathalie go past.

He went in and shut the door behind him.

'What do you want to do?'

'Nothing. Don't take any notice of me. If you're worried I'll pinch her trinkets, you can follow me . . .'

He began with the left wing, inspecting the rooms occupied by the young woman. He even went to the trouble of looking in the closets, which made Claire smile.

'Why do you think she'd hide in a cupboard?'

'It's as good a place as any.'

'She has no reason to hide.'

'Nor did she have any reason not to go out of the main entrance . . .'

He wandered around the drawing room, examined one

by one the portraits of stern-faced ancestors and thought about the life their descendant had led. Outside their portrait gravitas, might they not have done likewise?

'Where is the back entrance?'

'I may as well tell you, because it's hardly a secret.'

'Via the courtyard?'

'No. To the right of the lift there's a little glazed door that leads to a flight of steps down to the garden. Across the garden there's a gate in the wall which opens directly on to Rue Saint-Simon.'

'And this gate isn't locked?'

'It is. But as Monsieur and Madame Sabin-Levesque are the owners, they have the key.'

'Where is this key?'

'I don't know . . .'

That was an interesting question. Was it Gérard or his wife who had the key? And, if it was him, when had she taken it?

He went into the lawyer's small study and sat down in a comfortable leather armchair.

'Do you plan to stay here for long?'

'Until your employer comes back.'

'She won't be happy.'

'Why not?'

'Because you're not supposed to be here in her absence.'

'You're very devoted to her, aren't you?'

'Why wouldn't I be?'

'Does she treat you well?'

'She can sometimes be very nasty, unfair and aggressive, but I don't hold it against her.'

'Do you feel she is not responsible for her actions?'

'At those times, yes.'

'Do you think she is ill?'

'She can't help it if the only solace she was given was alcohol.'

'If she were to ask you to lie for her, to commit perjury, would you?'

'Without hesitation.'

'It can't be very pleasant when she vomits in her bed at night . . .'

'Nurses have worse than that to deal with.'

Maigret thought he heard a noise coming from the hallway. He didn't move, however, and the maid appeared not to have noticed.

'What would you say if I were to start screaming and accused you of trying to rape me?'

Maigret couldn't help laughing.

'It's an experiment worth trying . . . Let's hear you . . .'

She shrugged and walked off in the direction of the large drawing room and the other wing. She did not return; it was Nathalie who came teetering across the room.

She was ashen, with dark circles under her eyes, making her lipstick appear even more vivid, like a wound. She nearly fell over as she entered and Maigret rose to assist her.

'Don't worry about me. I can still stand up straight . . .'

She sank into the armchair that matched the one in which Maigret was sitting. She looked at him with a sort of stupefaction.

'Who told you . . . ?'

She shook her head, as if to erase the words she had just spoken.

'Press the button by the door to the drawing room.'

He did so. That button must ring a bell in the pantry.

'It's hot . . .'

Without getting up, she took off her brown tweed jacket.

'Aren't you hot?'

'Not for the time being. You probably walked too fast.'

'How do you know I was on foot?'

'Because you knew that I'd have traced the driver of your taxi and found out where you went . . .'

Still looking dumbfounded, she did not appear to be fully herself.

'You're clever . . . But you're horrible . . .'

He had rarely seen a woman so distraught, reduced to such a state as this. Claire knew why she'd been summoned because she was carrying a tray with a bottle of brandy, a glass and a packet of cigarettes . . . She filled the glass herself and held it out to her employer, who nearly knocked it over.

'You don't want one, do you? You're not an alcoholic yet . . .'

She could barely form the word, and repeated it.

'Has your doctor ever advised you to seek treatment?'

'Him! If I were to listen to him, I'd have been put away in a psychiatric hospital a long time ago . . . Which would have suited my husband . . . You see how unpredictable life is—'

She stopped abruptly, as if she'd lost her train of thought.

'Unpredictable . . . unpredictable,' she repeated, her eyes vacant. 'Oh yes . . . Life . . . My husband's the one who's dead and I'm the one who's alive . . .'

She looked about her and turned towards the drawing room. Her face suddenly lit up with a sort of satisfaction. Then she drank, and said, in a mournful voice:

'This is mine.'

He was expecting her to slither to the floor, but, despite her drunken state, she maintained some grip on reality.

'I never used to come in here . . .'

Now, she was gazing at the walls of the study.

'He only came in here to read.'

'Do you remember Chez Mademoiselle?'

She gave a start and her gaze became steely again.

'What did you say?'

'Madame Blanche, the owner of Chez Mademoiselle—'

'Who told you?'

'It doesn't matter. I have an excellent photograph of you and Gérard cracking open a bottle of champagne. It was before your marriage . . .'

She sat absolutely still, on the defensive.

'You never were a secretary. One of the places you worked in was a third-rate nightclub in Nice, and you were forced to go upstairs with the punters . . .'

'You are a bastard, inspector.'

And she drained her glass in one gulp.

'I am now Madame Sabin-Levesque—'

He corrected her:

'Widow Sabin-Levesque . . .'

She breathed haltingly.

'I don't suspect you of having killed your husband . . .
Despite all your energy, you are not physically capable of
it . . . Unless an accomplice—'

'I didn't even go out that evening . . .'

'The 18th of February?'

'Yes.'

'You remember it?'

'You're the one who mentioned that date . . .'

'Who telephoned you this morning?'

'I have no idea.'

'Someone wanted to see you at all costs and told you it
was vital . . .'

'Probably a wrong number.'

'You hung up, suspecting that the line was being tapped,
but, as if by coincidence, you went out this afternoon . . .
You didn't use the main door but the little garden gate . . .
By the way, which of you had the key?'

'Me.'

'Why?'

'Because he never went into the garden and sometimes,
in the summer, I would go and sit there. I'd hidden the
key in a crevice in the wall.'

'And did you use it?'

'To go and buy cigarettes over the road, yes . . . And
even to go for a drink in a bar . . . They'll tell you . . . I'm
the neighbourhood drunk, aren't I?'

'Where did you go this afternoon?'

'I walked.'

'And where did you stop?'

'I don't know. Maybe in a bar.'

'No.'

She was wavering and in the end he felt sorry for her. He stood up.

'I'm going to call your maid and she'll help you into bed.'

'I don't want to go to bed.'

The thought seemed to frighten her. She was living a nightmare which it was impossible to enter.

'I'll call her anyway . . .'

'No . . . Stay here. I'd rather you were the one to stay with me . . . Aren't you some kind of doctor?'

'No . . .'

'Give me your hand . . .'

She placed it on her chest where her heart was pounding rapidly.

'Do you think I'm going to die?'

'No. What is the name of your doctor?'

'I don't want to see him either . . . He'll have me put away . . . He's a very bad man . . . A friend of Gérard's . . .'

He flicked through the phone book and found the name and address of the doctor, who lived round the corner in Rue de Lille.

'Hello . . . Doctor Bloy . . . ? Inspector Maigret here . . . I am at the home of Madame Sabin-Levesque . . . She does not seem at all well and I think she needs you . . .'

'Are you sure she's not putting on an act?'

'Is that what she usually does?'

'Yes. Unless she's blind drunk . . .'

'I think it's the latter, today . . .'

'I'll be right over.'

'He's going to give me another injection,' she moaned.

'He gives me one every time he comes . . . He's an idiot who thinks he's cleverer than everyone else . . . Don't go. Don't leave me alone with him . . . He's a bad man. The world is full of bad people and I'm all alone . . . Do you hear me? . . . All alone . . .'

She started to cry and tears rolled down her cheeks. Her nose was running.

'Don't you have a handkerchief?'

She shook her head and Maigret gave her his, as if she were a child.

'Whatever you do, don't let him send me to hospital . . . I don't want to go there under any circumstances . . .'

It was impossible to stop her drinking. She would suddenly grab the glass, and next moment it would be empty.

The doorbell rang, and then Claire showed in a very tall man, built like an athlete, who, Maigret would later learn, was a former rugby player.

'Delighted to meet you,' he said, shaking Maigret's hand.

He glanced at Nathalie with indifference. She did not move and stared at him in terror.

'So, the same thing again? Let's go into your bedroom . . .'

She tried to protest, but he took her hand, his doctor's bag in the other.

'Monsieur Maigret . . . Don't let him send me . . .'

Claire followed them. Maigret didn't know what to do with himself and he eventually sat down in one of the armchairs in the large drawing room, which the doctor would have to walk through.

It took a lot less time than he had expected. The doctor came back, with the same detached expression on his face.

'This must be the hundredth time,' he said. 'She should be in a private hospital, for some time at least.'

'Was she already like that when Sabin-Levesque married her?'

'Not as seriously. But she had a drinking habit and couldn't go without. At first, there was a business with a dog that terrified her, and the fact was that the animal bared its teeth whenever she went near it or Gérard . . . She had the chauffeur fired and changed drivers two or three times, as she did her maids . . .'

'Do you think she's mad?'

'Not in the true sense of the word. Let's say neurotic. As a result of drinking like that . . .'

The doctor abruptly changed the subject.

'Have you found out who killed poor old Gérard? . . . My parents lived in the neighbourhood and we used to play together in the Luxembourg Gardens . . . We were at the same lycée, and then at university together . . . He was the finest man there was . . .'

They went down the stairs still chatting and stood outside on the pavement together for a while.

6.

Maigret walked along the embankment gazing absently at the Seine, his pipe in his mouth and his hands in his pockets, looking very much out of sorts.

He couldn't help feeling guilty. He'd been harsh, almost pitiless with Nathalie, even though he felt no animosity towards her.

Especially today. She was lost, incapable of playing her part to the end, and suddenly she'd caved in. He could tell that it wasn't an act, that she had no strength left. All the same, he'd done his job, convinced it was the right thing to do, and, if he'd been somewhat cruel, it was because he believed it was necessary.

Besides, the doctor, who'd known her for a long time, had barely been any less hard on her.

Now she was in a deep sleep, induced by the injection. But what about when she woke up?

There was only one person in that vast apartment who was devoted to her, Claire Marelle, her maid. And that was the way things had been for fifteen years.

The cook, Marie Jalon, who had almost brought up Gérard Sabin-Levesque, had always considered her an intruder. Honoré, the manservant, viewed the procession of bottles with distaste. There was a cleaner who came every morning and whom Maigret had only glimpsed, a certain Madame Ringuet, and he suspected that she too was on Gérard's side.

The lawyer was one of those people who retain a child-like quality all their lives and, because of that, are forgiven everything. In Gérard Sabin-Levesque this quality was a profound selfishness, combined with a degree of innocence.

Before his marriage he was already leading the life he would resume a little later. In his law firm, he was the golden boy who was successful in everything. And, in the evenings, when the fancy took him, he became Monsieur Charles.

He was known in most of the nightclubs around the Champs-Élysées. But curiously, there was no trace of him in Saint-Germain-des-Prés or Montmartre. He only hunted, so to speak, in a specific area, the classiest and most elegant.

The moment they spotted him, the liveried doormen would say respectfully, with a hint of familiarity:

'Good evening, Monsieur Charles . . .'

And, for a large part of the night, he'd be Monsieur Charles, an eternally youthful man, who smiled at everyone and handed out generous tips.

The hostesses would watch him, wondering if that night would be their turn. Sometimes he was content just to drink a bottle of champagne with one of them. Other times, he would leave with the girl, but the owner didn't dare raise any objection.

He was a happy man. A man with no problems. He didn't socialize among his own circle. He was never seen in the salons. He liked the easy-going hostesses and, when he spent a few days with one of them at her place, he enjoyed helping her with the day-to-day household chores.

He was certainly not looking to get married. He felt no need for a live-in wife in his apartment.

And yet, he'd married Nathalie. Had she acted all sweet and docile, the helpless little woman, with him? It was likely. In her passport photo, she had the touching expression of a vulnerable little girl.

She'd placed herself under his protection. She'd made him feel big and strong . . .

She had worn a white wedding dress, like a proper young lady, and on entering the apartment on Boulevard Saint-Germain she had been overawed. In Cannes too, the vast 1900s-style villa had felt like a paradise and she'd begun to put up with a dog that wasn't hers and that snarled at her.

What had caused the rift?

She was alone in the huge apartment for days on end. Her father-in-law and Gérard were downstairs, each in his office, and mealtimes were rather awkward. She didn't yet have Claire, but a maid for whom she was merely the boss's wife.

Gradually, she'd grown tougher. To start with, she'd demanded that her husband get rid of the dog, and he had done so reluctantly. In the evenings, they had nothing to say to each other. She didn't read. She simply watched television.

They still slept together, without any real intimacy developing between them.

And, one fine day, Gérard had gone out, without saying

anything, to visit the Étoile district and play his part as Monsieur Charles.

That was his true nature, his childlike side. He was full of life. Everyone welcomed him, celebrated him.

Whereas she'd believed she would become the heart of the home, she was in fact nothing but a useless accessory. He tolerated her. He didn't speak of divorce, but they were already sleeping in separate bedrooms and she moped in her bed, brooding endlessly over her resentment.

The air was mild. The sun was setting slowly in the west and Maigret walked without hurrying. Twice, he bumped into someone coming towards him.

As a hostess, she already drank, but in moderation. In the loneliness of the apartment, she began to drink more, to dull her senses.

Was Maigret mistaken? That was how he pieced together the past. The more she drank, the more her husband distanced himself from her.

Her father-in-law died. Gérard had additional responsibilities and had an even greater need to relax.

They had held out for fifteen years, both of them. And that was what astonished Maigret. For fifteen years, they had crossed paths in those rooms where no one really lived. In the end, she was no longer able to sit across the table from him.

She had become a stranger and had been lucky enough to find Claire, who had become her sole ally.

Why didn't she leave? Why did she put up with this suffocating existence?

She went to the cinema in the afternoons. Or at least

that was what she claimed. From time to time she had the chauffeur drive her to a bar near the Champs-Élysées where she drank, alone, perched on a high stool.

Without being asked, the bartenders refilled her glass as soon as it was empty. She spoke to no one. No one spoke to her. As far as other people were concerned, she was 'the woman who drinks'.

Had she at last met a man who cared about her, who made her aware of her worth?

So far, the investigation had not suggested that possibility. Vito stated that she always came out from the various bars she visited on her own, a little unsteady on her feet.

Now, she was a widow. The apartment, the firm and fortune awaited her, but was it too late? She was drinking more than ever. She was afraid of something. She seemed to be running away from reality, from life.

Where had she gone when she'd slipped out via the little garden gate? And who had telephoned her that morning?

With her, it was hard to differentiate between the truth and the lies. She was a skilled actress who, in the space of a few minutes, had transformed herself into a socialite to meet with the journalists and photographers.

Maigret walked halfway across Pont-Neuf and stopped at the Brasserie Dauphine.

'A pastis, like the other day?'

'No. A brandy . . .'

It was a challenge. He was imitating her. He was drinking brandy. And the first mouthful burned his throat. Even so, he ordered another before heading to the Police Judiciaire.

A file was waiting on his desk, the same one that he had gone through with his colleague from the Vice Squad.

He picked it up and took it into the inspectors' office. There were about twenty men in the room.

'I need ten of you, those who look the least like police officers . . .'

There were smiles, some of them tight-lipped.

'Here's a list of all the cabarets and nightclubs in Paris . . . You can ignore Saint-Germain-des-Prés and Montmartre. Concentrate on the eighth arrondissement and the surrounding area . . .'

He gave the list to Lucas along with a dozen prints of the Cannes photograph.

'You don't need to disguise the fact that you're police officers, but all the same, try not to be too conspicuous . . . Each one of you will be given a photograph and a number of addresses . . . Visit them at around midnight . . . Question the bartender, and possibly the owner, the maître d' and the hostesses . . . Remember the date of the 18th of February . . . Remember the name Monsieur Charles as well . . . I was forgetting that there are also the flower-sellers, who go from club to club . . . I know it would be a miracle, but I'd like to find out if anyone saw Monsieur Charles on the 18th of February . . .'

He handed the file to Lucas and went back into his office, still looking thoughtful.

It was perhaps a complete waste of time, but sometimes people remember a date because of a birthday, or a chance incident.

Lapointe had followed him.

'May I, chief? . . . I wanted to let you know about a phone call that came in for you while you were out and that I took the liberty of answering . . .

'It was from the Municipal Police. Puteaux informed them that one of their officers, intrigued to see a black Citroën parked by an area of wasteland for several days, had filed a report.

'Apparently there are bloodstains on the passenger seat, or rather on the seat back . . .'

'Who does the car belong to?'

'A certain Dennery, a civil engineer who lives in Rue La Boétie.'

'When was the car stolen?'

'That's the interesting point: on the 18th of February . . . He reported the theft to his nearest police station . . . No one thought of that deserted area of Puteaux . . .'

'Have the number plates been changed?'

'They haven't been touched. Which is why the owner could be traced straight away . . .'

'Where is the car?'

'I asked the Puteaux chief inspector to leave it where it is guarded by an officer . . .'

At last, a concrete clue! Small, granted, but which might possibly lead somewhere.

'Put me through to Doctor Grenier . . .'

So long as he wasn't in the middle of an autopsy!

'Grenier? Maigret here. I need you.'

'Now?'

'As quickly as possible . . .'

'A new body?'

'No. But the car that transported a body, by the look of things.'

'Where do I have to go?'

'Come over here. I don't know exactly where the car is; we'll call into Puteaux police station, they have the information.'

'All right. Give me fifteen minutes.'

Then he called Moers, in Criminal Records.

'I need your experts, the ones who dealt with the lawyer . . .'

'They're here. Where do you want them to go?'

'To Puteaux police station where they'll be told the location of the vehicle.'

Maigret forgot the difficult afternoon he'd just had. He and Doctor Grenier got into a police car, and Lapointe took the wheel and drove them to Puteaux, which, at that hour, was no small thing.

'It's rare to see you here, inspector . . .'

'I'd like one of your men to drive us to the vehicle that has just been found.'

'That's easy.'

He gave instructions to an officer who squeezed into the little police car with some difficulty.

'It's a stone's throw away . . . On a demolition site . . . They're knocking down an old ruin to build social housing . . .'

The car was covered in dust. The tyres and headlamps had been stolen. An officer was pacing up and down and a man in his fifties rushed over to Maigret.

'Do you see the state they've left it in?'

'Are you the owner?'

'Georges Dennery, civil engineer . . .'

'Where was the car stolen from?'

'Opposite my home. My wife and I were having dinner, and we were going to drive to a cinema in the Latin Quarter . . . But the car had gone . . . I ran to the police station . . . Who's going to pay for new tyres and headlamps and cleaning it up?'

'You will have to apply to the appropriate department.'

'And which is the appropriate department?'

Rather irritated, Maigret admitted:

'I have no idea.'

The interior was upholstered in a grey fabric which had soaked up the blood. The forensic pathologist took some little phials out of his bag and embarked on a complicated task.

The team from Criminal Records looked for fingerprints on the wheel, the brake handle and gear stick as well as on the doors.

'Have you found any?'

'There are some good prints on the wheel. The others aren't so clear . . . Someone smoked Gitanes, because the ashtray is full of butts.'

'What about the passenger side?'

'Nothing. Blood on the back of the seat.'

The doctor spoke up.

'And fragments of brain,' he added. 'Those are precisely the traces that would have been left by the man I autopsied . . .'

They worked for another hour, meticulously. A group

of curious bystanders had formed and two local police officers were keeping them at bay.

The car was parked halfway on to the demolition site, which seemed abandoned for the time being.

Monsieur Dennery went anxiously from one man to the other, concerned only to know who would pay for the repairs.

'Aren't you insured against theft?'

'Yes, but the insurance companies never pay out the full amount . . . and I don't want to end up out of pocket . . . If the streets of Paris were better policed, this wouldn't happen—'

'Had you left the keys in the car?'

'I couldn't imagine that someone would use it . . . All the seats need to be re-covered . . . I even wonder whether my wife will want to get into a car that has transported a body . . .'

The forensics team had found a few wool fibres which seemed to have come from a tweed jacket.

'I'll let you carry on, boys. Try to send me a preliminary report by tomorrow morning, even if it's incomplete.'

'We'll do our best, chief.'

'As far as I'm concerned,' said the doctor, 'it will be done quickly. A simple blood test. I'll call you at home this evening.'

Lapointe dropped Maigret outside his apartment building. Madame Maigret came to greet her husband at the door and looked at him with a frown.

'Not too tired?'

'Very tired.'

'Is your investigation moving forwards?'

'Possibly . . .'

He was gloomier than ever and appeared not to notice what he was eating. After dinner, he sank into his armchair, filled a pipe and watched television.

He was thinking about Nathalie.

Maigret was dozing in his armchair when the telephone rang, cruelly shattering the silence in which he was immersed. There was only one lamp on. The television had been switched off. Madame Maigret was nearby, sewing.

She never sat in an armchair, claiming that it made her feel trapped.

He lumbered over to the phone.

'Detective Chief Inspector Maigret?'

'Speaking, yes.'

His voice must have sounded gruff, because the caller asked:

'Am I waking you up?'

'No. Who is this?'

'Doctor Bloy. I am at Boulevard Saint-Germain, where Madame Sabin-Levesque has just tried to commit suicide.'

'Is she in a serious condition?'

'No. I thought you'd like to see her before I give her a stronger injection.'

'I'll be there right away . . . Thank you for letting me know . . .'

His wife was already holding out his jacket, and she went to fetch his overcoat.

'I suppose you're going to be quite a while?'

'Call me a taxi . . .'

While she was telephoning, he filled a pipe and poured himself a little glass of plum brandy. He was distressed, Madame Maigret could tell. He didn't have all the facts about what had happened, but he felt he was partially to blame.

'The taxi will be here in a minute . . .'

He kissed his wife. She went to the door with him and opened it. Leaning over the bannister, she watched him go down the stairs. And he gave her a little wave.

Two minutes later, a taxi drew up outside the building. He was about to give the address where he wanted to go when the driver said with a twinkle:

'Quai des Orfèvres?'

'No. Not this time. Boulevard Saint-Germain. Number 207a.'

One of the illuminated clocks they passed showed that it was 10.20. Without realizing it, he had slept for almost two hours!

He paid the taxi-driver and rang the main bell. The retired police officer came and opened the door.

'I don't know what's happened, but the doctor's up there.'

'He's just phoned me.'

Maigret went up the stairs two at a time and Claire Marelle let him in.

Doctor Bloy was waiting for him in Gérard Sabin-Levesque's little study.

'Is she in bed?'

'Yes.'

'Is her condition a cause for concern?'

'No. Luckily the maid once worked for a doctor and she immediately made a tourniquet above the wrist, even before calling me . . .'

'I thought the injection was supposed to knock her out until tomorrow morning, if not longer . . .'

'So it should have done. I don't understand how she could have woken up, got out of bed and moved around the apartment . . . The maid has set up a bed in the boudoir so as not to leave her alone. When she woke up with a jolt, she saw her employer walking past like a ghost – those are her words – or a sleepwalker . . .

' "She crossed the big drawing room, the dining room, and went into her husband's apartment . . .

' " 'What are you doing, madame? You must go back to bed . . . You know what the doctor said . . .'

' "Her mouth was contorted in a sort of twisted smile.

' " 'You are a good girl, Claire . . .' " '

The doctor added:

'Don't forget that at that point, the lights weren't on, other than in the boudoir. The scene must have been frightening, but the girl didn't lose her head.

' " 'Give me a drink.'

' " 'I don't think I should.'

' " 'In that case, I'm going to get the bottle . . .' "

'Claire thought it best to pour her one. She got her mistress back into bed, then telephoned me. I was playing bridge with friends and came racing over. The wound is deep and I had to apply three staples . . .

'She didn't say anything to me. She stared at me, her face blank, or rather, indifferent.'

'Does she know that you called me?' asked Maigret.

'No. I phoned from the study . . . I thought you might like to talk to her before I send her into a deeper sleep.

'This woman is extraordinarily resilient.'

'I'll go in and see her.'

Maigret made his way back through the apartment and entered the boudoir, where the camp bed still bore the imprint of a body.

'You see what you've done?' said Claire, without anger but in a sad voice.

'How is she?'

'She's lying absolutely still, gazing at the ceiling, and she won't answer when I talk to her. Please just be kind to her . . .'

Maigret felt awkward entering the bedroom. The covers were drawn up to Nathalie's chin, and her bandaged arm lay on top of the sheet.

'I thought they'd call you . . .'

She spoke listlessly.

'I really wanted to die . . . It's the only solution, isn't it . . . ?'

'Why?'

'Because I no longer have any reason to live.'

Maigret was struck by the words, because they didn't seem to chime with reality. There was no love, not even the semblance of a friendship, between her and her husband.

So he had never been her reason for living.

'I know you were only doing your job, but you were cruel . . .'

'Do you have something to tell me?'

She didn't reply straight away.

'Pass me the bottle . . . Once the doctor's given me the injection, it will be too late . . .'

He hesitated and then picked up the bottle from the chest of drawers.

'No glass. My hand's shaking too much and I'll knock it over . . .'

She drank from the bottle and it was a sorry sight, in that bedroom where everything was luxury and sophistication.

She nearly dropped it on the bedside rug and Maigret caught it.

'What are you going to do with me?'

Was she in full possession of her faculties? Her words, which she spoke in a dull, choked voice, could be interpreted in different ways.

'What do you hope for?'

'Nothing. I have nothing left to hope for. I don't want to be alone in this huge apartment any more . . .'

'It's yours now . . .'

Her mouth contorted again.

'Yes . . . It's mine . . . Everything's mine . . .'

There was a painful irony in those words.

'Just think if someone had predicted that when I was a little hostess . . .'

Maigret said nothing and didn't even think of taking his pipe out of his pocket.

'I am Madame Sabin-Levesque!'

She tried to laugh but only managed a sort of strangled sob.

'You can leave me now. I promise I won't try to kill myself again . . . Go home to your wife . . . Because you're not alone, are you . . . ?'

She turned her head a fraction to look at him.

'You have chosen a nasty profession, but it's probably not your fault . . .'

'Have a good night . . .'

'Don't be afraid. This time Doctor Bloy is going to increase the dose and goodness knows when I'll wake up . . .'

'Goodnight, madame . . .'

Maigret tiptoed out, rather as if leaving a death chamber. Claire was waiting for him in the boudoir.

'Did she talk to you?'

'Yes.'

'Did she tell you any secrets?'

'No. Is the doctor still in the study?'

'I think so.'

Maigret joined him.

'Over to you . . . I'll wait here . . .'

Maigret filled his pipe and sank into the armchair. A few moments later, Claire came into the room. She seemed less antagonistic towards him.

'Why are you so harsh with her?'

'Because I am convinced she knows who killed her husband.'

'Do you have proof?'

'No, I don't have proof. If I did, I would already have arrested her.'

Strangely, the girl did not protest.

'She's an unhappy woman.'

'I am aware of that.'

'Everyone in the household hates her, except me.'

'I am aware of that too.'

'When Monsieur Gérard married her, it was as if she'd stolen someone else's place.'

'Did you ever accompany her on her outings?'

'No.'

'Do you know where she went?'

'To the cinema.'

'Did you find cinema tickets in her bag or in her pockets . . . ?'

It was obvious that she had never asked herself the question.

'No,' she replied at last, after thinking for a moment.

'Did she spend a lot of money?'

'Monsieur Gérard gave her everything she wanted. She would tell me to prepare one handbag or another and to put a certain sum of money in it . . .'

'How much, for instance?'

'Sometimes a few hundred francs, sometimes two or three thousand . . .'

She bit her lip.

'I shouldn't have told you that.'

'Why not?'

'You know better than I do . . . She hardly bought anything from the shops . . . She had the tradesmen come here . . . She only went to the hairdresser's in person . . .'

The doctor came into the study and spoke to the maid:

'This time, I think you can sleep soundly . . . I gave her a dose that is used in sleep treatments . . . Don't worry if she doesn't wake up tomorrow morning . . . I'll drop by just before midday.'

'Thank you, doctor.'

She left the room and the doctor sat down, crossing his legs.

'Did she tell you anything of interest? In the state she's in, people sometimes say more than they intend to . . .'

'She asked me, among other things, what I planned to do with her.'

'She's just asked me the same question.'

'I think she knows a lot about her husband's death.'

'In any case, she's fiercely hiding something. That's why she's in the state she's in. I'm surprised she hasn't become hysterical . . .'

'She asked me for a drink and she was so insistent that I passed her the bottle.'

'You did the right thing . . . Given the point she's reached . . .'

'Medically, what's going to happen to her?'

'She will increasingly lose control of herself.'

'You mean she'll go mad?'

'I'm not a psychiatrist. As a matter of fact, in a day or two, I'd like a psychiatrist to examine her . . . In any case, if she carries on drinking as she does, she won't last long . . . She can't stay here where I don't have the necessary facilities to treat her . . . She needs to be in hospital . . . Not necessarily a psychiatric hospital . . . We'll get her sober and give her the rest she needs . . .'

He sighed.

'I don't like looking after this sort of patient . . . By the way, do you know when the funeral will be?'

'I haven't dared talk to her about it . . .'

'Do you think she'll want a chapel of rest?'

'The chief clerk will probably take care of it. She's in no state to do so.'

'The less disruption to the household, the better for her. I can't imagine a bier in the entrance hall or in the big drawing room . . .'

They both rose and said goodnight once out in the street. Maigret went home to bed. He slept badly, had nightmares. When his wife woke him with his cup of coffee, he ached all over as if he'd been making a great physical effort.

'Lapointe?' he asked on the telephone. 'Is he there yet?'

'He's just come in.'

'Put him on, Lucas.'

'Yes, chief?' said Lapointe.

'Come and pick me up at my place. But first of all, check whether there's any news.'

He washed, shaved, dressed and swallowed two aspirin tablets, because he had a pounding headache. He barely touched his breakfast.

'I'll be glad when this case is over,' muttered Madame Maigret. 'You're taking it so much to heart that you'll end up making yourself ill . . .'

He looked at her sullenly and tried to give her a smile.

'The newspapers are hardly mentioning it any more . . . Why's that?'

'Because there's nothing to say about it at present . . .'

He found Lapointe at the wheel of the little police car and slid in beside him.

'Nothing on my desk?'

'A report from forensics . . . The wool fibres found in the vehicle match those of the dead man's jacket.'

'What about the men I sent into the nightclubs?'

'Monsieur Charles was known to nearly all of them and he was thought of as a decent fellow . . .'

'The 18th?'

'None of the bartenders, maître d's or hostesses remember that night in particular. Jamin might have come across something. An elderly flower-seller, who goes from club to club in the area. For her, the 18th of February is important because it's her daughter's birthday. She states that Monsieur Charles, who always bought flowers from her, was at the Cric-Crac, in Rue Clément-Marot, that night . . .'

'Did she say anything else?'

'He was with Zoé, and he gave her red carnations.'

'Did they get her address?'

'Jamin wrote it down. She insists on coming to see you because she met you in the past, when you were in Traffic . . .'

They had reached the entrance which Maigret was beginning to know well.

'Shall I wait for you?'

'No. Come with me.'

He greeted the concierge in passing and went into the office waiting room. The receptionist let him through and he crossed Sabin-Levesque's office to enter Lecureur's. The latter stopped dictating, signalled to his secretary to leave the room and stood up to shake Maigret's hand.

'I hear she tried to commit suicide and that the doctor came last night?'

'Nothing serious. She's asleep . . .'

'Why do you think she did that?'

'If I knew, the investigation would quickly be over. What arrangements have you made as regards the formalities?'

'The will is going to be read this afternoon at three o'clock. I more or less know the content since I signed it as a witness. Madame Sabin-Levesque inherits his fortune, the villa in Cannes and the profits from the firm . . . The Chamber of Notaries will give a ruling on my case. Sabin-Levesque has expressed his wish for me to succeed him . . .'

'There is another urgent matter to settle: that of the funeral.'

'The family has a vault in Montparnasse Cemetery.'

'That's a good thing. We can't, in all decency, collect the coffin from the Forensic Institute and drive it straight to the cemetery. Madame Sabin-Levesque is not in a state to deal with it. Nor can I see a chapel of rest in the apartment upstairs.'

'Why not in the office?'

'That's what I was thinking. Would you make the necessary arrangements?'

'I'll telephone an undertaker's immediately. And I think we should send out an announcement to all the clients.'

'I think so too. Not to mention an obituary in the news-papers. By the way, have you been mobbed by the press?'

'Around a dozen reporters came asking indiscreet questions, and I threw them out. Two of them asked me how much Sabin-Levesque's fortune was worth . . .'

'Keep me posted about the funeral, but don't let anyone disturb Madame Sabin-Levesque.'

'Won't she go to the church?'

'I don't think so. It's up to the doctor.'

Since he was on the premises, Maigret went upstairs, followed by Lapointe. Claire opened the door to them.

'I had business downstairs and I wanted to know if everything was all right.'

'She's asleep.'

'Have you received any phone calls?'

'No. Only from a journalist demanding an interview and who was very annoyed when I said that wasn't possible.'

She was clearly tired. She couldn't have had much sleep.

Maigret turned to Lapointe: 'Drive me to Rue Clément-Marot . . .'

Just to have a look. At night, the street was almost empty. The nightclub door was half open.

Two cleaners were sweeping the floor strewn with streamers and confetti. The walls were covered in a brightly coloured fabric.

'What do you want? If you're looking for Monsieur Félix, he's not here.'

'Who is Monsieur Félix?'

'The bartender . . .'

A man came in, sure of himself.

'Well, well! Inspector Maigret . . . We had one of your men here last night . . .'

'What do you think of Louisa?'

'She's a former streetwalker who has virtually never left the neighbourhood. As she got older, she had to find a new job. Now she sells flowers in nightclubs . . .'

'Can she be trusted?'

'In what way?'

'She doesn't have too vivid an imagination? You can believe what she says?'

'Definitely. She can also keep a secret. Most of these girls have one, and she knows them all.'

'Thank you.'

'Why are you interested in her?'

'Because she claims to have seen Monsieur Charles, here, with a hostess, on the night of the 18th of February.'

'How come she remembers the date?'

'Apparently it's her daughter's birthday.'

'Then it must be true.'

The riverbank wasn't far away and a ramp led down to the river port.

7.

Maigret was having lunch with Lapointe in Place Dauphine again, but during the meal he barely said a word. He wasn't exactly gloomy, but there was a leaden air about him that Lapointe knew well. He was withdrawn, wrapped up in his thoughts.

When they arrived back at Quai des Orfèvres, they found an elderly woman sitting in the glass-walled waiting room and at first Maigret didn't recognize her. But she recognized him, and smiled at him through the glass.

It was old Louisa, as she was now called. He had known her when she was young and spry, one of the most beautiful ladies of the night on the Champs-Élysées.

He showed her into his office and removed his overcoat and hat.

'It's been a while, hasn't it, inspector! You were a young whippersnapper in those days and, once you'd caught me, I thought you were going to take advantage.'

'Have a seat, Louisa.'

'You've come a long way, haven't you! Mind you, I'm not doing so badly myself. And my daughter, even though she was brought up in the country, is now the wife of a debt collector for the Crédit Lyonnais . . . She has three children, which makes me three times a grandmother . . .

It's because of her, because of her birthday, that I remember the 18th of February clearly . . .

'First of all, there was a black car, with a man inside, about a hundred metres from the Cric-Crac. Then, inside the club, I saw Monsieur Charles sitting at a table with Zoé, the sweetest little thing . . . When I came out, the car was still there and behind the wheel there was still a man smoking a cigarette . . . It made a little glowing dot in the darkness . . .'

'Can you describe him?'

'It was too dark . . . I carried on with my round . . . I have my routine and I know my customers . . . I came back at around three o'clock . . . The car had gone . . . So had Monsieur Charles, and Zoé was with a great hulk of an American . . .'

'Do you know anything else?'

'I came here mainly because I wanted to see you again . . . Men are lucky . . . They don't age as quickly as us . . .'

The telephone rang and Maigret picked it up.

'Speaking . . . Yes . . . What? . . . A man killed, Rue Jean-Goujon? . . . Shot with five bullets in the chest? . . . I'm on my way . . . Inform the public prosecutor and Coindet, the examining magistrate . . .'

And to the elderly flower-seller:

'Thank you for coming. I have to go . . .'

'That's quite all right . . . I've seen you . . . That's enough.'

And, before leaving, she held out a timid hand.

'Lapointe! We're off again . . .'

In Rue Jean-Goujon, less than two hundred metres from the Seine, two police officers standing guard respectfully saluted Maigret.

'It's on the top floor.'

They took the lift. The door of one of the lodgings was ajar and Maigret shook hands with a local chief inspector who must have been a newcomer because Maigret didn't know him.

'It was the concierge who called us. She'd gone up to do the cleaning, as usual . . . When the tenant didn't answer the door, she used her master key to get in and that's when she discovered the body . . .'

A tall, youngish man, aged around thirty, was lying on the carpet, and a doctor was leaning over him.

It wasn't an apartment proper. The entire wall, on the street side, was glazed, and so was part of the ceiling, like an artist's studio.

'Do you know his identity?'

'Jo Fazio . . . He came from Marseille four or five years ago . . . Initially he was a pimp before finding a job as a bartender in a little, rather seedy club, the Paréo . . . He left around two years ago and, since then, it's not certain how he earned his living . . .'

The doctor stood up and shook Maigret's hand.

'It's strange. He was shot point-blank from a small-calibre gun, I'd even say with the barrel against his skin. I can see that two bullets perforated the left lung and there's another one lodged in his heart . . .'

The dead man's face had an expression of astonishment. As far as they could tell, he'd been a good-looking young man. He wore an elegant gaberdine suit of an almost luminous brown.

'Has the weapon been found?'

'No.'

The forensics team from Criminal Records arrived with their cumbersome equipment. Then it was the turn of the middle-aged deputy public prosecutor, who disliked Maigret but still shook his hand.

Examining Magistrate Coindet, however, was surprised.

'How come you asked for me to be appointed? Do you think this murder is connected with that of the lawyer?'

'It's a possibility. I was half expecting it. When Nathalie slipped out, yesterday, via the little garden gate, she had a purpose . . .'

He turned to Lapointe.

'Are you coming?'

There were too many people. He'd return when the experts and magistrates had left the scene.

He and Lapointe went into the concierge's lodge. She was a petite, lively brunette.

'How long had this Fazio lived up there?'

'Two years . . . He was a good tenant, quiet, who paid his rent on time . . . Because he was on his own, he asked me to clean his place and I'd go up every day at lunch time . . .'

'Was he usually home when you went up?'

'Most of the time no, because he ate at a restaurant . . . I didn't always see him leave . . . I'm very busy . . . The residents come and go and I don't take any notice . . .'

'Did he have a lot of visitors?'

'No. Only a lady . . .'

And she spoke the word respectfully.

'Every day?'

'Almost every day.'

'At what time?'

'Around three o'clock in the afternoon.'

'Did he come in with her?'

'No. He was up there first.'

'Describe her to me.'

'She was a real lady, you could see that straight away. In the winter, she wore a fur coat and she had at least three. In the summer, she usually wore a suit from one of the top couturiers . . . I know a bit about these things—'

'Her face?'

'It's hard to say . . .'

A marmalade cat rubbed itself against Maigret's legs.

'Young?'

'Neither young nor old . . . She could have been pretty . . . She must have been once . . . I'd say around forty, but her face was ruined . . .'

'What do you mean by ruined?'

'She nearly always had dark rings under her eyes, her features were drawn and her mouth had a strange pout . . .'

'Did she speak to you?'

'No. She'd go straight up.'

'Did she stay long?'

'She'd leave at around half past five.'

'By car?'

'No. I noticed she came by taxi, but she got out at the

corner of the street so no one knew where she was going . . .'

Maigret took the Cannes photo out of his pocket and showed it to the concierge, who went to fetch her glasses from the next room.

'Do you recognize her?'

'I'm not sure. This woman's very young and doesn't have the same mouth . . . But overall the face is the same . . .'

Maigret then showed her the little passport photo.

'What about this one?'

'That's better . . . With twenty years' difference between the two . . .'

'Do you recognize her, though?'

'I think so . . .'

The local chief inspector walked past the lodge. Maigret ran after him.

'Was the doctor able to extract the bullets?'

'That's the job of the forensic pathologist, who's not here yet . . . I think they found one that had glanced off a rib . . .'

'Would you go and fetch it, Lapointe?'

And, after thanking the inspector, he went back to the concierge.

'Did your tenant work?'

'I don't think so. Apart from mealtimes, he didn't go out at a regular hour . . .'

'Did he get back late at night?'

'I suppose I have to tell you everything?'

'It will be better for you, because you'll be cited as a witness.'

'Apart from the three o'clock lady, as I called her, he had

a much younger and prettier girlfriend . . . She generally arrived alone, or with him, at around two or three in the morning and spent the rest of the night up there . . . Once, I heard him call her Géraldine . . .'

Maigret was impassive. He looked as if his mind were blank.

'Do you know where she lives?'

'No. She probably works around here, because they always came home on foot . . .'

Lapointe had returned with the bullet. Maigret thanked the concierge and left.

'Where to now?'

'To Gastinne-Renette's . . .'

He was the gunsmith who usually acted as an expert for the Police Judiciaire. The assistant who was in the shop went to fetch his employer.

'Well, well! Maigret . . .'

They had known each other for over twenty years.

Maigret held out the bullet.

'Can you tell me off the top of your head what kind of gun this comes from?'

Gastinne-Renette put on his glasses, like the concierge.

'You know, this isn't what you could call an expert report. I'd need longer. It's clearly a small calibre, for example a Browning 6.35 that's made in Belgium. There are models with a mother-of-pearl grip. I sold one that was inlaid with gold to a woman customer—'

'Is it lethal?'

'Not from a distance. Further than three metres and the shot lacks precision . . .'

'The doctor reckons that the shots were fired right against the skin . . .'

'In that case, of course . . . How many shots?'

'Three or four, one to the heart and two others which went through a lung . . .'

'Someone really wanted him dead . . . Who's the victim?'

'A certain Jo Fazio, former bartender turned gigolo . . .'

'Pleased to have seen you again. Shall I keep the bullet?'

'I'll tell the pathologist to send you the others.'

'Thank you . . . and happy hunting . . .'

Maigret did not laugh at the joke but gave a wan smile.

8.

On the ground floor, the men from the undertaker's were transforming the lawyer's office into a chapel of rest, draping the walls with black fabric. The coffin had been placed in a corner, as if no one knew what to do with it.

'Is the body inside?'

'Of course . . .'

Jean Lecureur came out of his office.

'The funeral will be at eleven o'clock tomorrow,' he stated. 'The church is almost opposite. The announcements have been sent. Do you think Madame Sabin-Levesque will attend?'

'I'm certain she won't.'

'It's probably for the best. How is she? I have no news of what's happening upstairs . . .'

'Doctor Bloy must have come to see her before lunch . . . I'm on my way up there now . . .'

On the stairs, he said to Lapointe:

'Make sure you note down everything that's said.'

'Yes, chief.'

It was the manservant who opened the door.

'Where's Claire?'

'In the boudoir, I think . . .'

She came out to meet them.

'Is she asleep?' asked Maigret.

'No. Since the doctor left, she's been sitting on the edge of the bed, in her nightdress, and she hasn't said a word to me. She refused to have her bath and she wouldn't let me do her hair . . .'

'What did the doctor tell you?'

'Nothing much. To keep an eye on her.'

'Has she eaten?'

'No. She only answers by nodding or shaking her head.'

'What about you, have you had lunch?'

'I didn't have the stomach for it. I feel as if I'm watching a person slowly die . . . What's going to happen, inspector? Apparently the coffin's downstairs . . .'

'That's correct . . . Before going to see her, I'd prefer it if you could get her to put on her dressing gown.'

'I'll certainly try.'

Claire was no longer hostile towards him. He could tell she was confused. The two men stood waiting in the drawing room for a long time. After a quarter of an hour, Claire came to fetch them.

'She's in the boudoir. I was forced to give her her bottle.'

Maigret went in first. Nathalie was slumped in her usual wing chair, clutching the bottle of brandy. Her gaze was steadfast, however, and her face almost peaceful.

'May I?'

She pretended not to have heard, and Maigret sat down facing her. She caressed the bottle as if it were her most precious possession.

'I have come from Rue Jean-Goujon,' he said softly, as if not to alarm her.

At last she opened her mouth and said only one word, with indifference:

'Already!'

After which, she swigged from the bottle, as Maigret had seen her do before. A little colour rose to her pallid cheeks and her mouth began to twitch again.

'I suppose it no longer matters, does it?'

'You were afraid that, if he was arrested, he'd inform on you as his accomplice, weren't you?'

She shook her head in denial.

'No . . . It's worse . . . He asked me to come to his place yesterday and he demanded a very large sum of money, promising that after that he'd go back to Marseille and leave me alone . . .'

'Did you love him?'

She said nothing and her gaze expressed a profound despair.

'Why, if you loved him, did you take a gun with you?'

That seemed to distress her.

'I never had any illusions about him . . . He was my last chance . . . Don't you understand anything . . . ?'

She tried to light a cigarette but failed, because her hand was shaking. Maigret leaned forwards and held out a lit match. She did not say thank you.

'You have always felt superior to others, haven't you?'

She corrected him in a dull voice:

'I am proud. Or rather, I was . . . Now . . .'

She didn't finish her sentence.

'You found working in a nightclub demeaning and you

would have felt even more humiliated behind the counter of a department store . . .'

She listened to him. The minute he started talking about her, she began to take an interest.

'Sabin-Levesque fell in love with you . . . It didn't take you long to find out who Monsieur Charles was.'

Still tense, she didn't bat an eyelid.

'You hoped for a glittering life of luxury, cocktail parties, receptions, dinners.'

'I soon found out that he was the most selfish man I'd ever met.'

'Because you weren't the centre of his attention?'

She seemed surprised, and Maigret went on:

'He was everything and you were nothing in this household.'

Her gaze had become steely again.

'Everyone hated me, except Claire.'

'Why didn't you ask for a divorce?'

She looked about her as if that gaze encompassed the entire apartment, the entire home, the entire fortune of the Sabin-Levesques.

'Because you were greedy . . . You didn't care if he went off with pretty girls from time to time. You were Madame Sabin-Levesque . . . and you intended to remain so, whatever the cost . . .'

She drank. It had become an automatic gesture.

'You resorted to brandy. I suppose you also had lovers . . . ?'

'Flings . . . Men I met in bars . . .'

Now she'd cracked, she no longer thought to defend

herself. It was as if she felt a sort of pleasure in laying herself bare.

'Hotel rooms . . . Some got the wrong idea and wanted to give me money . . .'

She grimaced.

'Two years ago, you met Jo Fazio . . .'

'That was different. I love him . . .'

'He was a bartender . . .'

'I rented a studio apartment for him and I kept him . . .'

Again, she was cynically throwing down a challenge.

'At the point to which I'd sunk, I couldn't hope that he'd love me for myself. . . He pretended, and I pretended to believe him . . .'

'Who suggested doing away with your husband?'

'I believe we both thought of it.'

'Fazio identified the clubs frequented by the so-called Monsieur Charles . . . He followed him several times while waiting for the right opportunity to present itself . . .'

She shrugged. It was so obvious!

'One night, when your husband came out of the Cric-Crac, Jo Fazio took advantage of the fact that the street was empty and hit him over the head. He bundled him into a stolen car and transported him to the banks of the Seine. Then he abandoned the car on a demolition site in Puteaux . . .'

'I didn't have anything to do with those details.'

'But he telephoned you to tell you it was done?'

'Yes.'

'What life would you have led with your former bartender?'

'I didn't think about it.'

'Admit that it's not out of affection for your lover that you had him kill your husband.'

'I don't know any more.'

'You had to remain Madame Sabin-Levesque . . . Now you were the real mistress of the house . . .'

'You think badly of me, don't you?'

'Yes. At the same time, I can't help feeling sorry for you, because you are both tough and fragile . . .'

'Fragile?' she sniggered.

And Maigret repeated:

'Fragile, yes.'

'I assume you're going to arrest me?'

'It's my duty. Go and get dressed. Keep an eye on her, Lapointe, because I don't want her slipping out through the garden gate again.'

Maigret slowly filled his pipe, lit it and began to pace up and down. He waited for almost half an hour. When she came back, she had Claire in tow carrying a pigskin suitcase.

Before leaving the apartment, Nathalie took another long slug of brandy.

'They won't give me any in there, will they?'

She would be found guilty, it was certain. But given her sorry condition, she would probably be taken to the prison infirmary.

The law firm's door was open. The men from the undertaker's had finished hanging their drapes. She took a couple of steps forwards and looked at the coffin.

Her face showed no emotion.

'Is he in there?'

'Yes. He's being buried tomorrow.'

'And me, today . . .'

They put her suitcase in the boot and Maigret sat next to the prisoner. She stared out at the quays, the bridges, the pedestrians, the buses and the cars as if all that already belonged to a distant past.

On arrival at the Palais de Justice, Lapointe carried the suitcase, which was too heavy for her. Maigret knocked on Coindet's door.

'She's all yours . . .' he said morosely.

He looked at her, but he had already ceased to exist for her. She sat down facing the magistrate before being invited to do so, and appeared to be very much at ease.

INSPECTOR MAIGRET

OTHER TITLES IN THE SERIES

MAIGRET AND THE KILLER
GEORGES SIMENON

'*Leaning on the banisters, Madame Maigret watched her husband going heavily downstairs . . . what the newspapers didn't know was how much energy he put into trying to understand, how much he concentrated during certain investigations. It was as if he identified with the people he was hunting and suffered the same torments as they did.*'

A young man is found dead, clutching his tape recorder, just streets away from Maigret's home, leading the inspector on a disturbing trail into the mind of a killer.

Translated by Shaun Whiteside

INSPECTOR MAIGRET

OTHER TITLES IN THE SERIES

MAIGRET AND THE WINE MERCHANT
GEORGES SIMENON

'Maigret had never been comfortable in certain circles, among the wealthy bourgeoisie, where he felt clumsy and awkward . . . Built like a labourer, Oscar Chabut had hauled himself up into this little world through sheer hard work and, to convince himself that he was accepted, he felt the need to sleep with most of the women.'

When a wealthy wine merchant is shot in a Paris street, Maigret must investigate a long list of the ruthless businessman's enemies before he can get to the sad truth of the affair.

Other Titles in the Series

MAIGRET AND THE LONER
GEORGES SIMENON

'People who have been here a long time have been talking about him. This morning, when I was having my coffee and croissants, it was all they were talking about. The old folks, even the middle-aged people, remember him and can't understand how he could have become a tramp. Apparently he was a good-looking man, tall and strong, who had a good trade and made a very decent living. And yet he vanished overnight without saying a word to anyone.'

The death of a homeless man in a condemned building in Les Halles leads Maigret on the trail of the vagrant's mysterious past, and an event that happened years ago in the close-knit community of Montmartre.

Translated by Howard Curtis

INSPECTOR MAIGRET

OTHER TITLES IN THE SERIES

MAIGRET AND THE INFORMER
GEORGES SIMENON

'You see, I mainly work at night. I've ended up getting to know everybody. They're used to me in Pigalle. I exchange a few words with this person or that person. I go into the bars and cabarets where they give me a quarter bottle of Vichy without waiting for me to order anything.'

An anonymous tip-off regarding the death of a restaurant owner sends Maigret into the world of the Parisian nightlife, a notorious criminal gang and a man known as 'The Flea'.

Translated by William Hobson

OTHER TITLES IN THE SERIES